Blaze

Alaska—the last frontier.

The nights are long. The days are cold.

And the men are really, really HOT!

Can you think of a better excuse for a trip up north?

Don't miss the chance to experience some

Alaskan Heat

Jennifer LaBrecque's new sizzling miniseries:

Northern Exposure—
(October 2010)

Northern Encounter—
(November 2010)

Northern Escape—
(December 2010)

Enjoy the adventure!

Dear Reader,

Welcome back to Good Riddance, Alaska, where everyone is invited to leave behind what troubles them. This small outpost in the Alaskan bush is similar to many towns I discovered when I was lucky enough to visit Alaska years ago.

Nick Hudson is a world traveler who writes a travel blog about places off the beaten path. Sophisticated, yet down-to-earth and sincere, Nick shows up in Good Riddance to cover their pre-Christmas celebration activities. Only, he finds far more than he bargained for when he catches a glimpse of Augustina "Gus" Tippens, the Paris-trained chef who owns the local eatery. Nick and Gus learn that though love doesn't always take the traditional path, it's always worth savoring....

I hope you enjoy their *Northern Escape*. Writing these books has definitely made me think about going back....

I love to hear from readers. Please visit me at www.jenniferlabrecque.com.

Happy Holidays!

Jennifer LaBrecque

Jennifer LaBrecque

NORTHERN ESCAPE

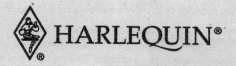

TORONTO • NEW YORK • LONDON
AMSTERDAM • PARIS • SYDNEY • HAMBURG
STOCKHOLM • ATHENS • TOKYO • MILAN • MADRID
PRAGUE • WARSAW • BUDAPEST • AUCKLAND

Recycling programs
for this product may
not exist in your area.

ISBN-13: 978-0-373-79585-7

NORTHERN ESCAPE

ABOUT THE AUTHOR

After a varied career path that included barbecue-joint waitress, corporate numbers cruncher and bug business maven, Jennifer LaBrecque has found her true calling writing contemporary romance. Named 2001 Notable New Author of the Year and 2002 winner of the prestigious Maggie Award for Excellence, she is also a two-time RITA® Award finalist. Jennifer lives in suburban Atlanta with a Chihuahua who runs the whole show.

Books by Jennifer LaBrecque

HARLEQUIN BLAZE
206—DARING IN THE DARK
228—ANTICIPATION
262—HIGHLAND FLING
367—THE BIG HEAT
401—NOBODY DOES IT BETTER
436—YULE BE MINE
465—HOT-WIRED
499—RIPPED!
537—BLAZING BEDTIME STORIES, VOLUME V
     "Goldie and the Three Brothers"
570—NORTHERN EXPOSURE
575—NORTHERN ENCOUNTER

1

A MOOSE WEARING A SANTA costume and hat, complete with beard, stood next to a Christmas tree adorned with moose ornaments. Where had they found a life-size plush moose? Journalist Nick Hudson looked around the airstrip office, soaking up the atmosphere. He liked Good Riddance, Alaska already. It was just what he'd hoped for and just what his blog readers would eat up. Quirky. Different.

It might be colder than a witch's tit in a brass bra, the sun had already made its brief appearance for the day, and though it was snowing outside it was cheery and toasty in here. The mingled aromas of fresh-brewed coffee, cinnamon rolls and wood-smoke scented the air.

An assortment of photos covered the wood walls. Lace-trimmed flannel curtains hung at the windows. Two old men with gray beards and baseball caps sat arguing over a chess board next to a potbellied stove. On the television set in the corner, Elvis crooned "Blue Christmas."

"Okay, Mr. Hudson—"

He turned back to face the woman at the airstrip desk. "Please call me Nick."

"Okay, and I'm Merrilee." Before she'd had to field a phone call, she'd introduced herself as Merrilee Danvers Weatherspoon, the airfield and bed-and-breakfast operator, as well as the town founder and mayor.

Nick estimated she was in her mid-to-late-fifties and still carried a surprisingly Southern accent, considering she'd told him she'd been in Alaska for twenty-five years.

"Let's get you checked in and I'll show you to your room," she continued. "We're delighted you decided to join us for our Chrismoose Winter Festival." Her warm smile exuded gracious charm.

"I'm excited to be here."

"Do you know how Chrismoose began?" she asked, clearly eager to relay the story.

"Just in bits and pieces," he said. A friend of a friend of a friend had mentioned it to Nick, which was why he'd decided to come to cover it in the first place. Juliette, the bush pilot who'd ferried him in from Anchorage, had given him a little more to go on, but he still didn't have it all straight.

"It's not real complicated, but it does make a good story," she said with another smile. "There was a hermit named Chris, no one ever knew his last name, who lived out in the bush. He'd come into town about every four months for supplies. When he did, he kept to himself. He just showed up, got what he needed, and left. About fifteen years ago, when our little town was really starting to grow and expand, it was two days before Christmas and we all about dropped our jaw when Chris came riding into town on a moose."

"He was *riding* a moose?"

"I wouldn't have believed it if I hadn't seen it with my own eyes. He'd found an orphan and raised it as a pet. Anyway, here he comes, wearing a Santa costume, riding through the middle of town on a moose with a bag strapped on its back."

"That must've been a sight to see."

Merrilee led him over to the wall of photographs. There in the midst of the mix was a color photo of a man in a Santa outfit on a moose. It was one of the craziest things Nick had ever seen. He grinned. "That is something else."

"Yessir, it was. And that bag on the back? Chris had carved wood toys for the children in town. He said he wanted to make sure the kids all had a Christmas, in case Santa couldn't find us out here. Every year, he'd show up and it wasn't just the kids who looked forward to it. Then one year Chrismoose day came and went and no Chris and no moose. We had a rough idea where he lived so a few of us drove out to check on him. We found him dead. We figured he'd probably passed a couple of months before. In the spring, when the snow melted, we found the moose dead, too. Because Chris had kept it as a pet and fed it, once Chris was gone it didn't know how to survive on its own. We never did find out who Chris was or if he had any family. We buried him but thought it was a shame such a wonderful tradition should die with him so our Chrismoose celebration was born. Eventually, it turned into a full-blown winter festival."

"That's a great story," Nick said.

Merrilee looked pleased with his reaction. "It is, isn't it? Now we draw quite a crowd every year. When you walk around town, you'll see all the campers and RV's parked on the outskirts of town. We get folks coming in from as far as five-hundred miles away."

"Awesome."

"You'll find a schedule of events in your bedroom and all the businesses in town have them posted in their window." A frown wrinkled her forehead. "Unfortunately flu season has hit early and we've got a bit of a situation going on. We're telling everyone to make sure you wash your hands often and keep them away from your face." She waved her hand in dismissal. "Now enough about that. How far have you traveled to join us? We like to track these things."

Before he could answer, a door set in the wall beneath a sign that read Welcome to Gus's opened and a ponytailed blonde came barreling through, only to stop short and gape when she saw him.

"Oh my God. Oh. My. God." She blinked as if she couldn't quite believe her eyes. "Are you Nick Hudson?"

Nick laughed. Sometimes people recognized him but it was usually in New York. He certainly hadn't expected to be pegged in a small Alaskan town. "I am." He held out his hand. "Pleased to meet you…"

"Teddy. Teddy Monroe." She shook his hand and then

just sort of held on. "I can't believe you're here. This is wild."

Nick gently disengaged his hand from hers.

"Okay. I guess I missed something," Merrilee said. "I didn't realize you were famous, Mr. Hudson."

"Please, call me Nick, and trust me, I'm not famous."

Teddy Monroe jumped in. "Oh, yes he is. He's only the most popular travel writer at the *New York Times*. He travels all over the world and specializes in blogging about places that are off the beaten path. Wow, you're going to blog about us, aren't you? This is so cool!"

He grinned at her enthusiasm. "I came for the Chrismoose celebration. I thought it'd make for some interesting articles."

"Really?" If Nick hadn't been so used to studying people and reading them, he would've missed the flicker of alarm in Merrilee Weatherspoon's eyes. "The *New York Times,* huh? That's impressive."

"It pays the bills."

"He's being modest," Teddy said. "He started working there right after college—" she looked at Nick for confirmation "—at least that's what it says on your bio page."

He nodded. "I was lucky. My parents owned a diner and the travel editor for the *Times* used to come in. He mentored me, got me an internship while I was in school, and the rest, as they say, is history."

"I'm not a stalker or anything," Teddy said. "I just love New York. It's my goal to move there next year and study acting."

"Teddy's our aspiring thespian and quite the New York fan," Merrilee said.

"Hey, my boss used to live in New York. You might've heard of her—she was a chef there before she moved here and took over the restaurant." She jerked her thumb over her shoulder in the direction of the door she'd entered through. "Gus Tippens."

It struck Nick as charmingly naive that this girl from a town with one street and no stop lights would think he might know one other person in a city of millions.

"New York's so big," Ms. Weatherspoon said with a tight smile. "I'd be surprised if Nick had heard of Gus."

"Her? Gus?"

"Short for Augustina," Teddy said. "Just like my name is short for Theodora." She rolled her eyes. "Why my parents had to name me after my grandmother…" She shook her head. "How you stick a baby with a name like Theodora is beyond me."

"Well, I'm sorry to say I've never heard of Gus but I'm looking forward to eating at her restaurant." His curiosity was piqued. "That sounds like a good story, in fact. You don't find many Big Apple chefs who move to the Alaskan wilderness and open a restaurant." It would make a great human interest angle, especially since it was a given some of his readers would recognize Gus's name or at least the restaurants in the city where she'd worked.

"And she trained in Paris," Teddy said, as if to ensure he was suitably impressed. He was.

"Did you come over for something in particular,

Teddy?" Merrilee said. He had a sense she was uncomfortable with the conversation.

Teddy looked sheepish. "Oh, yeah. Gus wanted me to check if her box of truffles came in on the flight."

"It sure did." Merrilee picked up a box from the corner of her desk and passed it to Teddy. "I was going to run them over as soon as I got Nick checked in."

Teddy backed her way toward the door she'd come through earlier. "Okay, then. I guess I'll see you tonight at dinner. I mean—not like that. It's just that, you'll be eating over here and that's where I work, you know, at the restaurant."

Nick was hard-pressed not to laugh but he didn't want to hurt the young woman's feelings. "Sure. I'll see you then."

She gave a little wave and pushed open the connecting door. For a brief second he caught a glimpse of a dark-haired woman with a shock of white in the front and he felt something of a shock himself. Striking. Arresting.

While the blonde had been nice, she didn't attract him. But that woman—he assumed she was Gus—well, she was a different story altogether. He was definitely looking forward to dinner tonight.

"WE'VE GOT TO FIGURE OUT something and figure it out fast," Merrilee said, trying not to panic, pacing back and forth in front of the counter of Bull Swenson's hardware store. She'd had to bide her time until he'd finished loading the final trim order for the almost-complete new community center.

Normally Merrilee found comfort in the smell of sawdust and lumber, but she wasn't feeling it now. She was too stinking worried.

Bull stroked his beard, a sure signal his wheels were turning. She'd fallen for Bull like a ton of bricks the first time she'd laid eyes on him twenty-five years ago. They'd been an item ever since.

Bull had repeatedly asked her to marry him and she'd repeatedly turned him down. When she'd left her husband in Georgia, she'd so desperately wanted to escape his cheating and lying ways that she'd packed her RV and driven as far away as she could. The day she'd wound up here, she'd known it was a special place. She'd found where she belonged.

And while she'd vowed to never marry again—and meant it, once had been enough—technically she also couldn't because her jack-ass husband wouldn't sign the divorce papers. She'd claimed to be divorced anyway because at first she'd thought it was just a matter of months until Tad relented and signed.

However, months had turned into years and then to confess the lie had become too awkward. Tad had shown up last month and finally signed, but once the truth came out, things just weren't right between her and Bull. He told her he loved her, but he'd also told her he wouldn't ask her to marry him again. The asking would be up to her.

She wondered if things would ever be right between them again. But Nick Hudson, with his New York connection and his blog, was far bigger trouble than her and Bull's strained relationship.

Bull finally spoke. "So, he writes for the *New York Times* and he's already said he wants to write about Gus?"

"Yep. All this time and now when she's starting to feel safe again, to get her life back, this guy could ruin everything for her." Merrilee rubbed at her temple, feeling sick inside. "What are we going to do? If he finds out the truth…" She couldn't suppress a shudder. Both Gus and Bull knew her opinion of reporters. They were snakes. Merrilee didn't trust a journalist as far as she could throw one.

"Where is he now?"

"He's out with Dalton looking around town. Dalton's grounded until his plane part comes in—"

"Oh, did Juliette fly him in?"

Merrilee paced back and forth, which she knew drove Bull crazy but she was too anxious to stand still. "Yeah." Dalton Saunders was the primary pilot who made the runs out of Good Riddance and Juliette Watson filled in when there was overflow or in a pinch like now when Dalton's plane was out of commission. "Anyway, Dalton stopped by the airstrip so I sent Mr. Hudson off with him. They were getting along like a house afire when they left."

She'd found that particularly annoying. She didn't like Nick Hudson. If she was honest, it wasn't the man himself, more the threat he posed to Gus, but nonetheless she found it galling that Teddy had acted the fool and then Dalton had been chummy. If it was up to Merrilee she'd stick his butt back on the next flight to Anchorage but it was a free country and she, unfortunately, couldn't run him out on the figurative rail.

She rubbed her fingers over her forehead in a futile attempt to ward off a headache. "I assured her she'd be safe here, Bull. I can't let her down."

It had been a terrible time. Gus had been a wreck when she'd arrived in Good Riddance. She'd been engaged to Troy Wenham, son of a prominent New York politician from a long line of prominent politicians. Wealth and power had crowned them minor royalty.

According to Gus, his family had disliked her intensely from the beginning, considering her a gold digger. Troy had become increasingly controlling and Gus had broken the engagement. Infuriated, Troy had refused to accept it.

Merrilee had never pressed for details but she knew Troy had begun stalking Gus. Going to the police had proven useless in the face of his family's power and influence.

She'd switched jobs and moved. He'd followed her by tracing her credit card usage and he'd threatened that she'd never be free of him.

It had taken careful planning but Lauren Augustina Matthews had dropped off the face of the earth. Troy had never found her here because Merrilee was unknown to him. Even though the story in Good Riddance was that Gus was Merrilee's niece, she wasn't. Gus's mother, Jenny, and Merrilee had been friends since childhood. Jenny had died before Gus and Troy had met.

Merrilee had been honored when Gus had contacted her for help. She'd assured Gus they'd keep her safe and help her start a new life in Good Riddance. But if Nick Hudson blogged about her or her restaurant in the *Times* all it would take was one sharp-eyed detective, or Troy himself, to put two and two together and once again he'd begin his terror campaign.

"Merrilee, the way I see it, she's got three choices." When Bull spoke, she paid attention. He'd spent two years in a Viet Cong prison during Nam. She had no idea what he'd been like before. All she could attest to was he was now a man who considered every angle and said nothing lightly. "We don't know this guy so trusting him with the truth is risky." She and Bull were the only ones privy to the real deal.

"We could kill him, but it's damn hard to get away with anything like that these days, plus he's just sort of stumbled into a situation, he's not here with malice." Bull was dead serious, which was just one of the things she loved about him. He weighed every course of action, even the outrageous ones. "And that leaves us with the third option, which isn't good, but about the only thing she can do is ask him not to mention her or her restaurant in his posts."

She rubbed at the throbbing in her right temple. "He's a journalist. That's just going to make him want to dig deeper. How much can he find out, do you think?"

Bull cocked his head to one side, considering, stroking his beard. "He'll probably figure out pretty quickly that's not her real name. It won't take much digging to find out I own the restaurant and bar, not her—that's a matter of public record, even though we've kept it quiet. Outside of that, I don't think there's much he can find."

"Why'd he have to turn up?" She was so frustrated with the situation she could scream. "Things were going so well for her."

Bull shook his head. "Come on, Merrilee. It was just a matter of time. Sooner or later everything comes to a reckoning." She knew he was referencing the recent showdown with her husband...well, now ex-husband. "Have you talked to her?"

"No. I came over here as soon as I got him out the door. I thought we should strategize first and then talk to Gus together. Although I'm sure she already knows because Teddy was gushing like a geyser." Teddy was something of a dreamer but Merrilee had never seen her gaga like that.

Bull pushed to his feet. "I'll put a sign on the door and we'll head over to Gus's so we're all on the same page."

"ARE YOU SURE YOU'RE OKAY, honey?" Merrilee said as Gus ushered Merrilee and Bull to her apartment door.

She was as okay as she'd been in the last four years. "I'm fine," she said. "Thanks for coming over. You two have been lifesavers. Good Riddance has been a lifesaver. I hope you know how much you mean to me." Her look encompassed both of them.

"We do and you know how important you are to us."

Gus nodded, her throat suddenly clogged with tears. They were as close to family as she had, with her mother dead and her father having checked out of her life when she was a kid. They'd become surrogate parents.

Merrilee caught Gus up in a quick hug. "It's going to be okay." She released her and patted her on the shoulder. "Just throw yourself into your work, honey."

"Shout if you need us," Bull said, his manner gruff as usual, but the caring in his eyes evident.

"I will."

They ducked out the side door of her apartment that lead to the outside rather than the stairs from the restaurant. She leaned her head against the door and the old feeling of being Troy's prey again threatened to swamp her. The truth of the matter was it was never gone, she just managed to hold it at bay most of the time. Regardless of how far she'd run, his shadow was always on her doorstep. The worst was when she went to bed at night, when her mind was no longer busy, when the nightmares could come to her in her sleep. Without a doubt she was stronger for the experience. But he'd scarred her, permanently marked her somewhere deep inside.

She'd never told Merrilee and Bull all of it. She'd never been able to bring herself to talk about coming home and finding her sheets slashed and covered in red paint that looked like blood. And still the police would do nothing. The Wenhams were to New York what the Kennedys were to Massachusetts.

Gus breathed in through her nose, employing the technique she'd learned in yoga years ago and which she now taught on Sunday afternoons for a small group here in Good Riddance. She focused on her inhalation and exhalation, finally managing to center herself.

Feeling calmer, in control, her thoughts turned to Nick Hudson. Her heart had dropped into her stomach when Teddy had come back over to the restaurant, truffle box in hand, dropping the bomb that a reporter from New York was next door. Gus even knew who he was—both she and Troy had loved Nick's travel pieces. They'd even tentatively tossed around a couple of different places Nick had written about as potential honeymoon destinations.

Nick's writing had been witty and insightful. Once upon a time, in her previous life in New York, she'd even fancied herself just a little bit in love with him, based on his writing. She'd had the somewhat whimsical notion a person's writing offered a glimpse into their soul and she'd liked what she'd seen of his. It hadn't hurt that he was gorgeous to boot, according to pictures of him online and in the paper.

She hadn't read one of his columns since she'd moved here. What was the point? That life was dead to her. Her passport, her driver's license were both useless, since they were in her real name. It had been too painful to read his columns or anything related to New York. Instead she'd immersed herself in her new world, thankful she'd found a haven and an opportunity to practice her craft.

Oh, yes, she'd known exactly who he was when Teddy imparted the news. And like an idiot, rather than her instincts of how much danger he posed kicking in, her initial gut reaction had been a frisson of excitement. Anticipation had trailed through her, reminding her she was a woman who'd been more than four years without a man. She'd had date offers since she'd been here but she simply hadn't been interested. However, one mention of Nick and that silly little crush she'd had years ago had reared its annoying head.

She shook her head. Her best course of action was to fly as far below his radar as possible. And with the influx of people here for the Chrismoose festival, she was going to be so darn busy that should be easy to do.

Squaring her shoulders and pushing away from the door, she headed downstairs. She had a restaurant to run.

2

NICK LAUGHED AS HE DODGED two kids playing a game of ice hockey using broomsticks and a chunk of ice for a puck. Beside him, Dalton Saunders grinned. "Everyone's pretty jazzed up for the festival. I'm sure it's nothing compared to New York but this is busy for Good Riddance."

"I like it. There's a good energy going on here. I've been some places where the people aren't as friendly and you just don't feel it."

"So what do you do when you turn up somewhere and it's a wash?"

"You think, oh, hell, I should've done better homework if I want to keep my job." Dalton chuckled. "No, seriously, I write it like I find it. I try to find at least one interesting angle to push. But readers want the skinny. Especially since I cover places off the beaten path, the traveler is usually forking over a little extra cash to get there. They want to know what to expect. If I've sugarcoated it and it's a wash when they get there, complaints are going to come in."

"I hear ya," Dalton said. "That's why we printed a schedule. It keeps getting bigger every year so we figured it was easier this way."

There were a whole lot of things going on over the next six days. Fireworks, ice fishing derby, dogsled races, cross-country skiing race, snowmobile races, a moose burger cook-off, arts and crafts show, Mr. Wilderness contest, and a Ms. Chrismoose pageant. Everything wrapped up with the Chrismoose parade and the dispensing of toys followed by a potluck dinner.

"At this point, our biggest problem is running out of places for people to stay. The B and B is full. I'm renting out the cabin next to mine to a couple from Anchorage. I know lots of people are staying with friends and family. When we get down to the other end of town, you'll see all the motor homes and trailers. It's hell on them getting here because those roads are rough."

Nick made a mental note. This was the kind of information he needed in order to write a thorough piece. He'd booked his room at the B and B months ago. He guessed it was a good thing he had. The place only accommodated three guest rooms and then there was Merrilee's private quarters. "Any plans to expand the B and B or build any rental cabins?"

"Merrilee or Bull would know more about that than I do. I do know a group from a big resort corporation came out last year. I flew them in from Anchorage." Dalton shook his head. "They were a bunch of suits. They looked around and met with the town council on building a spa resort here. The council turned them down. We're just not that kind of community."

Dalton pointed across the street. "Curl's place always raises a few eyebrows with the tourists."

Nick read the sign across the front window and chuckled. Curl's Taxidermy & Barber Shop & Beauty Salon & Mortuary. "That's definitely different."

"Yeah. He said he listed taxidermy first because that was his biggest draw."

Snapping a photo, Nick grinned. "My readers will love this."

"The rest is what you'd pretty much expect to find in any small town—Laundromat, dry goods store, hardware store, bank, engine repair shop, doctor's office." He canted his head to the left. "My fiancée, Skye, is the doc and I'd drop by and introduce you but I'll do you the favor of not taking you in there. There's a flu outbreak. Talk about some bad timing."

"That's what Merrilee said earlier." Nick could see the packed waiting room through the big glass window. "Yeah, I'll pass on going in there. I'll meet Skye some other time before I leave. Are you originally from Alaska?"

Dalton shook his head. "No. Michigan. I quit the corporate gig, got my pilot's license and moved here eight years ago."

"You obviously like it here."

"I wouldn't want to be anywhere else, especially now that I found Skye. There's nothing quite like having the right woman in your life. I don't know how to describe it except life's just better. It's like switching from a regular screen to high-definition television—everything's just a little brighter, clearer."

"That's cool. Congratulations." And he did think it was cool. It wasn't that he didn't want to settle down with someone, he'd just never met that someone. In his family everyone, his parents, his brother and both his sisters, swore they'd known within days they'd met the right one. He'd just never had that click. Hell, he hadn't had a date in months. He was tired of the whole dating game. The image of the woman he'd caught a glimpse of earlier, Gus, came to mind.

"Thanks," Dalton said. They continued walking until they reached a large wooden building across the street. "That's our new community center." To their left was an assortment of RV's and travel trailers. A number of dogs were outside several of the vehicles, obviously there for the dogsled race. "That's our softball field in the summer and our Chrismoose Festival parking lot in the winter." He grinned. "And thus concludes your tour of Good Riddance, Alaska."

"I really appreciate it."

"No problem. Hey, unless you just like to eat alone or you've made alternate plans, why don't you meet us for dinner at Gus's tonight? It'll have to be a little later than usual because Skye's so swamped at work—probably around seven."

"HE SHOULD BE HERE AT any time now," Teddy said, watching the door, fretting.

Gus considered it an exercise in supreme self-control that she refrained from strangling Teddy on the spot, although that would be inconvenient since they were serving dinner and Gus needed Teddy's help. They were slammed with the extra Chrismoose visitors in town. Gus couldn't run the kitchen, the bar, and the dining room alone. Otherwise…. Teddy's ongoing chatter about Nick Hudson was dancing on Gus's last nerve. The man could unwittingly pinpoint her for Troy. And maybe Teddy's starry-eyed enthusiasm reminded her too closely of herself years ago.

"Just relax, Teddy, and listen for the trumpets to sound, heralding his arrival," Gus said.

Teddy cut her eyes and looked sheepish. "Okay, I guess I have been going on about him, but we just don't get celebrities here in podunk Good Riddance."

It was on the tip of her tongue to point out writing for a newspaper did not make the man a celebrity, but then she dialed herself back. Teddy had no clue what Nick's arrival meant to Gus and under different circumstances, Gus would've been excited about meeting him, too. But there was a whole lot of water under *that* particular bridge. Gus garnished the two plates and handed them off to Teddy with a forced smile. "No, we don't get many celebrities here in Good Riddance."

She wiped her hands on her apron and turned back to the stove. The soothing smells and sounds of the restaurant washed over her. Regardless of how harried she was, there was a comforting familiarity to the clink of silverware against dishes and the sound of conversation and laughter at the different tables all set to a backdrop of music.

Gus was stirring the sauce burbling on the back burner, when someone other than Teddy heralded her from the service counter. "Hey, Gus."

Startled, Gus dropped her spoon, sending it clattering to the stove.

"Oops, sorry about that. I didn't think I'd scare you," Jenna, one of Good Riddance's newest citizens, said.

"No worries. I was just zoned out." Normally, it wouldn't have startled Gus. Her kitchen was an open-to-the-dining-room design and she loved it that way but she was definitely on edge tonight. "How's it going, Jenna?"

"Um, pretty good," Jenna said, glancing over her shoulder toward the front door, obviously looking for someone.

"Are you meeting someone?" Gus asked.

"No. I'm not waiting on anyone in particular."

Jenna had shown up with Merrilee's husband, now ex-husband, Tad as his fiancée. Jenna had, despite her airheadedness seen Tad for the creep he was, not to mention the cradle robber had been twice her age. She'd elected to stay in Good Riddance rather than go back to Atlanta and had started herself quite the thriving nail business over at Curl's.

"Could I help you with something, Jenna?" She liked Jenna but she was too busy tonight to stand at the counter chatting.

"Um." Jenna angled herself so she could talk to Gus and watch the doorway. "I just thought I'd tell you since the Ms. Chrismoose Pageant is coming up, I'll give you a mani/pedi for half price. Seeing as how you're the reigning Ms. Chrismoose, you want those nails looking nice when you hand off your crown…well, antlers or whatever they are."

"That's sweet of you to offer, Jenna—" the woman truly had a big heart "—but I don't think I'm going to have time and the kitchen's pretty rough on my nails. Manicures are usually a waste of time for me."

Jenna looked horrified. "But you can't hand off your crown with your nails looking like that. Sorry, but your cuticles are a hot mess." Gus glanced down at her hands. They weren't bad. Short but clean. Jenna leaned over the counter separating the kitchen from the dining room, and lowered her voice conspiratorially. "I want to keep it quiet because I don't want the other ladies to think that I have a big advantage over them in the pageant, but I have had some previous pageant experience."

Gus nodded solemnly. That was no shocker. The perfect makeup and shoulder-length blond hair bespoke a pageant history. "Okay. I'll keep it quiet."

"Thanks. So, you just can't go up there with those nails. And you'll want to rub a little Vaseline on your teeth beforehand to make 'em shine when you smile."

When hell froze over. The very thought almost gagged her.

"Thanks for the tip." It was impossible not to like Jenna—beneath those silicone breasts beat a heart of gold, just like now when she was all wigged out over Gus's plain nails—but sometimes it was hard not to gape in amazement at some of things that came out of her mouth. Since Jenna seemed in no hurry, Gus started inching her way back to the stove.

The front door opened and Nelson Sisnuket walked in. Nelson qualified as one of Gus's favorite people in Good Riddance. A native who wore his long, straight hair pulled back in a ponytail, he assisted Dr. Skye Shanahan. On Thursday night's he emceed karaoke at Gus's place. Nelson was good people. A shaman-in-training in his clan, there was always a good vibe rolling off of Nelson with his calm demeanor and wry humor.

He looked tired tonight but she knew he and Skye had been swamped with flu patients.

"Okay. Nice chatting with you. See ya, Gus." Jenna pushed away from the counter and timed it so that she nearly bumped into Nelson. "Oh…hey, Nelson. How's it going?" The blonde fell into step beside him.

Nelson sent a wave Gus's way. "It's going fine. How are you, Jenna?"

Gus double-checked to make sure her mouth wasn't hanging open. Jenna had been waiting on *Nelson?* Apparently so. Not that Nelson wasn't an attractive man—in fact, he was downright handsome—but Gus would've never pegged him as Jenna's type. And poor Jenna, if she was crushing on Nelson, and it looked as if she was, that dead-end street could only lead to heartbreak for her.

Interracial marriage wasn't widely accepted in Nelson's clan. His cousin Clint, a guide, had fallen in love with and was engaged to Tessa Bellingham, a white woman, but it had caused quite a stir with his family. Both Clint and Tessa had had to fight for Clint's grandmother to accept their relationship. That had been one thing, especially since Clint, even though he looked full native, was the product of an interracial marriage and subsequent divorce. But it wasn't a remote option for Nelson. As a shaman-in-training, it was out of the question for him to date outside his race and Nelson took his tribal responsibilities as sacred duty.

Gus didn't want to burst Jenna's bubble, but she'd talk to Jenna in the next day or so and just drop the information out there. Gus was nothing if not practical and in Jenna's shoes...well, Gus would want to know if she didn't stand a snowball's chance in hell with a particular man.

She understood Jenna's dilemma, though. Lately, Gus had become very much aware she'd been in a four-year sexual drought. The problem was none of the men in Good Riddance did a thing for her. As much as she liked Good Riddance, and she did, four years later and she still felt something like a fish out of water. And really that was just as well because if you started dating, or to be blunt, sleeping with someone in Good Riddance and things didn't work out, well it was going to be awkward bumping into one another afterward. And in a town this size, avoiding someone was nearly impossible. Not to mention keeping an affair quiet. Everyone in town would probably know before the act itself was even consummated.

She had placed two plates on the counter for pickup and had turned back to the stove to fill yet another order when the strangest tingling sensation swept over her, through her. She shook her head slightly. Perhaps it was some kind of weird static electricity... Dear God, don't let her be coming down with the flu. But this didn't feel like any flu she'd ever had before. She didn't feel achy, she simply felt tingly.

Behind her Teddy said, "Oh, you made it."

"I did." It was a male voice, rich like a mole sauce—dark, but not sweet, with velvety chocolate undertones. A faint shiver chased down her spine.

She knew. Before she even turned around, she knew she'd find Nick Hudson, the man who could wreck her world, on the other side of the counter.

Fixing a smile on her face, she turned…and nearly forgot how to breathe. Of course she recognized him. She'd seen his photos. A little age had settled well on him. His dark hair was shorter than in his photos and laugh lines fanned out from the corners of piercing blue eyes set in his lean, ruggedly handsome face, but he was familiar.

No, she recognized him on another level. Something snapped into place for her. A rush of sexual energy surged through her. She was looking at the man she wanted.

And he was the man she'd sworn to avoid while he was here.

NICK FELT AS IF HE'D BEEN slammed in the gut. He wasn't prepared for the impact of meeting her. He'd thought he was. He'd been sure of it. He was wrong.

He'd caught a glimpse of Gus Tippens earlier and had looked forward to meeting her, but….

She was an arresting study in black and white and shades in between. Her short hair was so dark it was almost black except for one chunk of pure white. Her eyes tilted slightly at the corners, giving her a faintly exotic look, which was furthered by eyes an unusual shade of gray, almost silver, fringed with dark lashes.

But it was her mouth that nearly did him in. She had a perfect bow of a mouth and she wore red lipstick. Beneath her apron, she wore trim black slacks and a white top. More striking than beautiful, something inside him responded in a way he'd never experienced before. It was like stumbling across an orchid in a field of daisies.

Teddy snapped him out of whatever the hell he'd fallen into with an introduction. "Nick, this is Gus Tippens. Gus, Nick Hudson."

"Hello," she said, her voice like water flowing over smooth stones. "I've certainly heard a lot about you."

"It's a pleasure to meet you," Nick said. "I've been looking forward to dinner. Your reputation preceded you. It smells great. My parents own a diner in New York so I've always appreciated good food and it certainly smells good." Dammit, he'd already said that. "I'm sure it will be good."

Okay, he was ready to kick himself in the ass. What the hell was wrong with him? He'd traveled all over the world. For the most part he managed some measure of sophistication but here he was babbling away like a spring brook.

Although she was friendly enough and offered another smile, he sensed a wariness in her. "Your reputation preceded you, as well. I hope you enjoy your meal." She turned to the other woman, clearly dismissing him. "Teddy, will you please seat Mr. Hudson?"

"Nick. Please call me Nick."

She nodded, a shimmer of a smile curving her red lips. "As you can guess, we don't stand on a lot of ceremony here in Good Riddance. Teddy, will you seat Nick?"

"Sure thing. He hung out today with Dalton so he's going to eat with the crew," Teddy said. "He just wanted to meet you before he went to the table."

"You're in good company, Nick. I hope you enjoy your meal. And now if you'll excuse me…." She turned back to her stove.

In the interest of not making a bigger fool of himself than he had up to now, he said to Teddy, "I see Dalton over there. It's no problem seating myself."

"Okay. I'll be right over in a sec to get your drink order."

It was cold outside and maybe a drink was just what he needed to get himself back on track. "No need to make an extra trip. Whiskey. Neat."

"Gotcha," Teddy said.

He made his way across the room to where three couples sat at two rectangular tables put together. The empty seat was on the side that afforded him a clear view of the room…and the kitchen. Once Nick was seated Dalton launched into the round of introductions.

The two native men were cousins. Clint Sisnuket worked as a guide, while Nelson Sisnuket was part of the local healthcare system. There was Dalton's fiancée, Skye Shanahan, a pretty redhead. Clint was engaged to Tessa Bellingham, the petite blonde next to him who'd just moved to town a couple of weeks ago after visiting to shoot video footage. And the statuesque blonde Jenna Rathburne was also a newbie and also obviously had a thing for Nelson.

"If you can't remember all the names, no worries," said Tessa. "We threw a lot at you."

Nick grinned. "I'm pretty sure I've got it." Teddy walked up and delivered his drink and took dinner orders. Nick had already learned that while a short-order cook worked from a standing menu for breakfast and lunch, dinner was prepared by Gus and she had two offerings to choose from each evening.

"A toast," Clint said, raising his glass in Nick's direction. "Welcome to Good Riddance where you get to leave behind what troubles you."

Everyone clinked glasses and drank.

Skye Shanahan looked across the table to him. "You're single, Nick?"

Dalton pretended outrage. "Woman, please. I'm sitting right here for crying out loud."

Skye shook her head even as Nick laughed and answered her question. "Yes. I'm footloose and fancy free."

Skye exchanged a look with Tessa. "Don't say we didn't warn you. I came to fill in for two weeks and here I am." She held up her hand with a sparkling engagement ring.

Tessa laughed. "Yep. I was only here five days and well…" She also held up her hand with an engagement ring attached.

"Not me," Jenna said, holding up her bare fingers. "I came with a fiancé, but I dumped him. Hey, if you wind up needing an engagement ring, I can make you a good deal on mine."

Laughing, Nick deliberately shifted in his seat,

playing to his audience. "I'll consider myself appropriately warned." He looked into the kitchen again, where Gus, her dark head bent, worked efficiently.

An hour later, after Nick had polished off what was some of the best food he'd ever tasted, Gus left the kitchen and began to make her rounds by the various tables. Crazily his heart began to beat faster the closer she came to their table, and he was increasingly challenged to follow the conversation going on around him. Finally, she stopped by their table. "Hi, guys. How was everything tonight?"

There was a chorus of *greats* and *outstanding*. Then she looked directly at him. "Was everything to your liking, Nick?"

The booze and the food had been some of the best he'd ever had. Instinctively he knew she'd probably be the best he'd ever had, as well. Feeling no more in control than when he'd met her earlier, he attempted what he hoped was a charming smile. "The best I ever had."

Her answering grin rocked through him. "I like hearing that. I also really like my privacy so I'd appreciate you not writing about me or my establishment." She plucked his bill up from the table and neatly tore it in two. "And tonight was on the house."

Son of a bitch. She'd been slick with backing him in that corner...and in front of a table full of witnesses.

He'd been intrigued when Teddy had first mentioned she'd moved here from New York. He'd been the other side of interested when he actually met her. Now she fascinated him.

He had to know more about this woman.

3

GUS FLIPPED THE OPEN SIGN TO Closed, ready to sag with exhaustion. They'd been busy and she'd been keyed up all night, even more so once she'd met Nick Hudson. It was as if she had an internal radar screen that kept him within view. She'd known where he was all night. And more than once she'd glanced his way, only to have those blue eyes of his snare her from across the room. Just a look from him and her pulse began to race.

"Thank God, it's closing time," she said to Teddy who had begun to turn the chairs upside down on the tables so they could sweep and mop. "I'm dead tired tonight."

"I'm pretty tired myself," Teddy said.

Gus paused, momentarily distracted from obsessing over Nick Hudson. It was unusual for Teddy to be tired. She was always a bundle of endless energy. For that matter, Gus was too, but she'd been so tense all afternoon and all the emotions around Troy that had come back—it had just exhausted her. Perhaps that was why she'd reacted so strongly to Nick.

In the kitchen, Gus began scrubbing down the stainless steel work surfaces. Teddy was uncharacteristically, but mercifully, quiet. Maybe she'd talked herself out earlier, going on nonstop about Nick.

Four long years. It had been four long years since Troy had totally stalked her, terrorized her to the point she thought she might have a nervous breakdown. Instead, she'd managed to finally get away from him with her life and a shock of white in her once dark hair, thanks to stress-induced alopecia. She'd lost a chunk of her hair and when it had grown back in it was stark white. Every day when she looked in the mirror, it served as a reminder of what could happen when you allowed a man to have control over you.

And for four years she'd not had an ounce, not even a smidgen of sexual attraction for a man. Was it irony, bad karma or just some wicked cosmic joke that one look at Nick Hudson and she'd tripped right into lust mode. Damn it to hell. She'd accomplished what she needed to accomplish tonight and now she just had to stay as far off of his radar as possible.

She ran hot water over a fresh kitchen cloth and began to rinse the area she'd just scrubbed. One look at him had her yearning for the slide of a man's fingers against her skin, the brush of masculine lips against the inside of her wrist, the back of her knee. Actually that was a lie because it wasn't just a yearning for any man, it was for *that* man.

Just because she'd been hard-pressed to think of anything other than what it would be like to kiss him, to wrap her arms around those broad shoulders, to feel the

scrape of his whiskers against her neck, her cheek…
well, that was all going nowhere because that definitely
didn't constitute staying off his radar. Nope, that would
be just plain stupid and Gus didn't do stupid.

"Gus," Teddy said from the opening leading to the
dining room. Gus glanced up and immediately noticed
Teddy's pallor, accentuated by two bright red spots on
her cheeks and her overly bright eyes. "I feel sick."

Teddy staggered to the sink and promptly threw up.
Gus tried not to gag. She'd never been very good at
handling someone throwing up. When Teddy finally
quit heaving, Gus passed her a towel. Teddy's teeth
began chattering and Gus pressed the back of her hand
to Teddy's face.

"You're burning up. You've got the flu."

"I don't think I can drive."

There was no way she'd let Teddy walk out the door
and even try it. "I know you definitely can't drive. I'll
drive you home."

Teddy shook her head no, still hanging on to the
edge of the stainless steel industrial sink, but adamant
nonetheless. "I appreciate it but you'll grind my gears."
Teddy drove a stick and the one time Gus had tried to
drive it had been a disaster. Gus didn't even own a car
anymore. She'd abandoned hers when Bull came for
her and she hadn't needed one since moving to Good
Riddance. "Call Marcia. She'll come get me."

Teddy lived on the outskirts of town with her older
sister, Marcia and Marcia's girlfriend, Sybil. Their mom
had died when Teddy was fourteen and her dad had
taken off for parts unknown a year later.

Gus rang Marcia and then bundled Teddy into her coat, gloves and hat. Poor Teddy sat huddled in her coat in a chair near the door while she waited, a bowl close by in case she had to throw up again.

Within minutes Marcia was there, concern for Teddy knitting her brow. "C'mon, baby, let's get you home." Marcia looked at Gus as she helped Teddy to her feet. "Sybil's driving Teddy's car home."

Marcia's demeanor was cool as usual when she spoke to Gus. Marcia blamed Gus for Teddy's determination to move to New York. And while Gus had never encouraged or discouraged Teddy's aspirations, she understood Marcia not wanting her only relative to move so far away. Gus was all too familiar with holidays, and regular days, spent without the one you loved most. Despite how she felt about Merrilee, she still ached for her mother, particularly at this time of year.

"Take care, Teddy, and feel better," Gus said before the door closed on the two sisters.

Poor Teddy. Weary, Gus looked around at the empty restaurant. Everything had to be cleaned again and sanitized tonight before she could go to bed. Flu germs and restaurant customers made a bad combination.

She straightened her back and took a deep breath. There was nothing for it but to do it. Sleep was overrated anyway.

Gus was just getting started when the connecting door between her place and the airstrip office opened and Merrilee came in.

"I thought I'd double-check on you." Merrilee glanced around the empty room. "Where's Teddy?"

"Sybil and Marcia just picked her up. Teddy has the flu."

Merrilee shook her head. "That's not good. Not good at all. You're gonna have to scrub down the entire place again, aren't you?"

"Everything has to be cleaned again, including all the place settings because we were both washing dishes tonight."

Merrilee began to roll up her sleeves. "Then let's get to it."

"Merrilee, you can't—"

"I most certainly can." Merrilee planted one hand on her hip. "I'm not leaving you to scrub this entire restaurant by yourself. We'll get it taken care of in no time working together. Now let's get cracking."

They'd worked their way through the dining room and moved on to the bar, sharing a tired but companionable silence, when Merrilee spoke up. "You better call Darlene Pritchford first thing in the morning, Gus."

Darlene had worked at the restaurant off and on for years. She wasn't as quick as Teddy but she'd always proven a good backup.

Gus shook her head. "I heard yesterday Darlene has the flu."

Merrilee winced. "I can waitress and bus the tables but I don't know what to do when it comes to the kitchen. You think Lucky or Mavis could stay over and help with some of the evening stuff?"

That wasn't an option. She shook her head. She wouldn't even ask it of her short-order cook who covered breakfast and lunch. "He's got family in from the lower forty-eight for Chrismoose and the holidays. He's already going above and beyond by not asking for any time off. I can't ask him to work extra hours. Mavis is busy with Chrismoose and her grandchildren. I'll manage." She wasn't sure how, but where there was a will, there was a way.

And there were benefits—she'd definitely be flying under Nick Hudson's radar since she'd be far too busy to do anything else. And exhaustion would hopefully keep at bay the specter of Troy…as well as the allure of Nick.

THE FOLLOWING MORNING NICK rolled out of bed and made short work of showering and shaving. He whistled beneath his breath while he dressed. Crossing to the window affording a view of Main Street, he pulled back the flannel curtain to check out what was going on.

It was still dark outside but that was no surprise in Alaska in the middle of December. Daylight hours ran short but he'd noticed yesterday that the town just rolled along, regardless of the dark. Several pickup trucks were already out on the street. A couple of dogs trotted down the sidewalk behind someone so bundled Nick couldn't tell if it was a male or female. Light glowed from behind windows and spilled out onto the snow from buildings lining the street.

He'd written his first blog post last night after dinner and checked his email before he headed downstairs. He had plenty of time. Clint Sisnuket had offered to take him out to the native village this morning but he and Clint weren't meeting up for nearly an hour.

He'd answered what needed addressing and signed out of his email when he decided to run a search on Gus. She'd asked him not to mention her or her establishment so he wouldn't but that didn't mean he couldn't find out about her. He wanted to know more and the internet was a damn good resource.

He typed in her name and hit Enter. Nothing. That was odd. Teddy had clearly said the woman had worked in New York. She should be referenced in some culinary capacity or as staff at some restaurant. He tried changing the spelling of the last name and came up with another blank. It simply made him more determined. He tried her name with key words such as *chef, food reviews* and *culinary arts* all coupled with *New York*.

Not a damn thing. Beginning to get frustrated and more determined than ever, he logged on to a site available to *Times* staff where anyone who'd ever breathed could be found since it searched a nationwide database of birth records. Bingo. Three Augustina Tippens.

Wait…no bingo. He did some quick math. One of them would be ninety-four if she was still alive. Another was six years old and the last Augustina Tippens was fifty-one.

What the hell? He did a public records search for Good Riddance. She ostensibly owned the restaurant and bar next door, but there was no business license or property deed in her name. There wasn't even a phone number listed for her in the white pages.

Whoever the hell she was, she wasn't Augustina Tippens. And she'd made no bones about it last night—she didn't want him mentioning her or her restaurant in his blog. Curiouser and curiouser.

Nick turned off his computer and headed downstairs. The B and B bedrooms were all located on the second floor above the airstrip office. Merrilee's voice drifted up the stairs.

"Teddy's got the flu and so does Darlene. Lucky's got family in from out of town so he's busy and can't stay for the evening shift. Gus is in a fix. I can pitch in and wait tables but I don't know what to do in the kitchen."

Nick entered the room just as Dalton responded, "That bites."

"Yeah, poor Gus." She looked over at Nick. "Good morning. How'd you sleep last night?"

Dalton nodded a greeting. "Nick."

"Good morning," Nick said, aiming the greeting at both of them. The two older men by the potbellied stove were busy arguing. Nick had a feeling they were nearly permanent fixtures in the airstrip office. "I slept like a log. That's one comfortable bed."

"I'm glad to hear it. How about a cup of coffee? Fresh brewed?"

She seemed a little warmer toward him today but he was sure he hadn't misread her reserve yesterday after Teddy had come over. It was yet another oddity, he noted. And coffee sounded good.

"I'd love a cup. Straight-up black, if you would."

Merrilee poured the brew into a thick ceramic mug and handed it over. "Thanks," he said, cupping his hands around the warm cup. "Did I hear you say Teddy's got the flu?"

Wrinkling her nose, she nodded. "Unfortunately, yes. After the restaurant closed last night, Teddy went home with the upchucks and a fever."

"That doesn't sound good." Nick sipped at the aromatic coffee. Strong and dark, it packed a wallop, just the way he liked it. "So, that leaves Gus shorthanded?"

Merrilee shook her head. "And then some."

An idea took hold. Actually, it was perfect. He wanted to find out more about her. Gus was shorthanded. He had grown up working in a restaurant. Gus had backed him into a corner last night with her power play. Fine. It was his turn to make her an offer she couldn't refuse.

Nick said to Merrilee and Dalton. "I'll be right back. I've always wanted the chance to be a knight in shining armor."

Before they could ask any questions, he turned on his heel and headed across the room. "Morning," he greeted the couple in the room next to his who had just come downstairs. He was pretty sure it took every ounce of Merrilee Weatherspoon's self-control not to follow him to see what he was up to. He might've just met her but he knew Merrilee liked being in the know.

When he entered the restaurant, Gus was in the kitchen talking to the cook. Lucky? Yeah, that was the guy's name. The place wasn't nearly as full as it had been last night, but about three-quarters of the tables were taken and about half the bar seats.

Nick leaned against the counter separating the kitchen from the rest of the room. Gus's back was to the room as she talked to the cook. This morning she wore dark gray pants with a lighter gray sweater. Rather than being formfitting, her clothes merely hinted at the curves underneath. Nick, however, had no trouble running with that hint.

Lucky nodded his head in Nick's direction and Gus turned. Faint dark circles were smudged beneath her eyes as if she hadn't slept well. Once again, wariness glinted in her grey eyes but there was also a glimmer of attraction. Whether she liked it or not, she was drawn to him. And he damn sure was drawn to her. It seemed to stretch between them and bind them together in the restaurant full of people. She could have been the only one present.

"Hello," she said. "Can I help you?"

"Morning," he said, saluting both Gus and Lucky with his coffee mug. He plowed ahead without giving her a chance to respond. "I understand Teddy's got the flu which leaves you shorthanded."

The wariness increased tenfold, but she nodded nonetheless. Gus Tippens was no dummy. She knew he was up to something. "Yes."

"I don't know if you remember but I mentioned last night that my parents own a diner. I grew up working in a restaurant and I know my way around a kitchen and a bar. I'll be glad to step in for Teddy."

Lucky smiled, looking damn relieved. "There you go, Gus. Problem solved."

For a second he caught a glimpse of panic before she banked it. "I can't let you—"

"No, no, no. I insist. I know how to take orders. As long as I can work it around covering the Chrismoose events, I'm yours."

She appeared less than thrilled at the prospect.

"I'LL BE IN THE STOCKROOM," Gus told Lucky as the connecting door closed behind Nick.

"Sure thing, boss," Lucky said, expertly flipping a pancake.

Gus closed the door behind her. She did some of her best thinking in here. She paced back and forth between the shelves stacked with jars and bottles. How could she refuse his help without looking like a total idiot for turning down assistance she desperately needed?

Then there was the not-so-inconsequential factor that all he had to do was walk in the room and she was all systems go.

She'd known he was behind her earlier, before Lucky had nodded. Gus had *felt* him as surely as if he had touched her. She'd simply hoped if she pretended she didn't know he was there he'd go away. Just having him on the other side of the counter set her to simmering. How in the heck was she supposed to work with him in her kitchen?

Damn him. He knew she was desperate, but desperation aside if he'd had a private conversation with her she could've turned him down. But no, just as she'd made her request to him last night in front of witnesses, he'd done the same to her this morning. She would look totally unreasonable, especially after Lucky had piped up as to what a great idea it was.

The stockroom door opened and Merrilee poked her head inside. Merrilee knew this was one of her thinking spots. "Lucky said I could find you in here. Mind if I join you?"

"Of course not. Come on in."

Merrilee stepped into what was becoming a very tight space with the two of them sandwiched in there between the shelves. Beaming, Merrilee announced, "I've got a surprise for you."

And for the second time that morning Gus had an unexpected announcement lobbed her way.

"You've done what?" Gus asked, not exactly incredulous, but yes, it was quite a surprise.

"I've set you up with Jenna for a manicure/pedicure this morning," Merrilee said, patting her on the shoulder. "With everything going on, I thought you needed a pick-me-up. And there just aren't that many opportunities to spoil a woman here."

It was on the tip of Gus's tongue to say she didn't have time and mani/pedis weren't her thing but then she reconsidered. Merrilee was so excited to be able to do something. She was a woman of action who needed to fix things. There was nothing she could do to get rid of Nick being here. Presenting Gus with this gift was about the only option available to Merrilee and whether Gus had the time to spare or not and regardless if it wasn't her thing, Gus wasn't going to rob Merrilee of the one way she felt able to make a difference.

Plus, sometimes you had to go with the flow. Just yesterday Jenna was going on about Gus's nails and now this. So she pasted on a smile and said, "Thanks, Merrilee. That's very thoughtful. When is my appointment?"

"Well, that's the thing. It's now. So Lucky and Mavis can run the show while you're gone." To steal one of Merrilee's expressions, she looked pleased as punch.

"Luellen canceled so Jenna can work you in if you can be there in ten minutes."

Gus smiled at how happy Merrilee looked, especially considering how miserable she'd been yesterday. "Then I'd better head her way since things are covered here."

She snagged her gloves, hat and coat.

"I hear you've got yourself a helper this evening." Merrilee snorted in disgust. "He overheard me talking to Dalton and he was over here in a flash and not a ding-dang thing I could do about it. He's a sneaky snake, that one. I'm sorry, Gus."

Shrugging into her coat, Gus said, "Don't worry about it. There was no way to get out of it." An idea presented itself and Gus offered an evil smile. "But he'll be sorry."

"Really?"

She made an executive chef decision. "Oh, yes. He's got a ton of onions to chop this afternoon."

Merrilee laughed and then sobered. "Just be careful with him, Gus. He's dangerous."

"Yes, I know." Merrilee would totally fall apart if she only knew just how dangerous, considering Gus had a heck of a time keeping her wits about her when he was around. Of all the men in the last four years, why him? Why now? Why the man who could, with one mention of her or her restaurant, tip Troy off to her whereabouts?

All she knew was he affected her in the most disconcerting way. Yep, Merrilee should be concerned. She tugged on her gloves and hat and they stepped out into the kitchen. "I'm running out for a bit," she said to

Lucky who could care less whether she went or stayed. Understandably, he liked to run his own kitchen during breakfast and lunch. He'd even talked to her about opening his own place in town but he wasn't sure Good Riddance could support two restaurants and he didn't want to cut into her business.

Merrilee patted her shoulder again. "Relax and enjoy. God knows you work hard enough."

"I will and thanks again." Impulsively she reached over and hugged the older woman.

"You're welcome, honey."

Merrilee headed back to the airstrip. With a wave toward Lucky, Gus left through the front door. She stepped out into the morning cold, hoping the walk from her place to Curl's would help clear her head.

Despite being up late last night cleaning—not nearly as late as it might've been without Merrilee's help— she'd awakened early this morning. She simply couldn't seem to help herself. Sitting in bed, she'd logged on to her laptop and looked up Nick's columns for the first time in four years.

He was still an excellent writer. His pieces displayed a wry sense of humor and painted a picture without being too lengthy, and he certainly had an eye for the unusual. Reading his column again made her long for a change of pace, something different. And she felt guilty as hell for even thinking that.

Good Riddance had proved a haven when she'd desperately needed one. Troy had been relentless in pursuing her. And—she could actually think about it now without going into full panic mode—he'd damn near raped her that last time he'd found her. She'd known then it was either take desperate measures to get away from him or one of them was going to die.

She loved the people here, although she'd never allow anyone to get too close. She was happy, but reading Nick's column made her long for New York's hustle and bustle. She missed more balanced seasons. She missed the outside world. And God help her, but she'd lain in her bed last night and realized just how much she missed sex.

Sex and travel and New York. The sex she could manage, not that she had yet, but it was doable. However, New York and travel were lost to her. It was too risky because the next time Troy found her, someone was likely to get seriously hurt and most likely she'd be the one who didn't fare well.

She drew a deep breath. She should be content with the life she had here. It was a good life and a good town. She smiled at the whimsical moose heads mounted on the electric poles. You didn't find those everywhere.

Good grief, she seriously needed to get out more. She hadn't seen Tessa's new sign in front of the video rental/ screening room she was pulling together in the center of town. Gus rapped on the glass window and Tessa looked up from where she was cataloging DVD's on a narrow shelf. Gus pointed to the sign above the door and gave a thumbs-up, mouthing, "Nice."

Tessa laughed and mouthed back, "Thanks."

Gus liked Tessa. She was genuine and it was nice to have another woman close to her age in town.

She crossed the street and entered Curl's Taxidermy

& Barber Shop & Beauty Salon & Mortuary. No doubt about it, Curl's was...unique. Up front were two barber chairs. Over to the left of the chairs, Jenna had set up a small table and on the floor was a foot spa tub. About a dozen bottles of different colored nail polish sat on one corner of the table. The front room was cramped quarters because most of Curl's business was done in the back. Gus sniffed. Curl's place always smelled faintly of formaldehyde. Come to think of it, so did Curl.

Donna and Jenna looked up, both greeting her with hellos and smiles.

"I'm almost done with Donna. Can you give me a minute?" Jenna asked.

"Sure thing," Gus said, shrugging out of her coat. She tossed her coat, gloves and hat in one of the two barber chairs up front and settled in the other.

A side door on the outside led to a large open room. That's where the dead bodies were delivered, be they human or animal form. Gus would never forget Elmer Watkins keeling over dead at the table within a month of her opening the restaurant. Bull, Dalton, Clint and Nelson had carried Elmer down to Curl's and put him out on a table in the back next to a table holding a bull moose that had been brought in for taxidermy. Curl had laid Elmer out in the back room in his best overalls and flannel shirt...and had put the bull moose standing at attention next to him, since they'd come in together and the moose hadn't yet been picked up. Everyone had commented on how natural both of them looked.

No doubt about it, Curl could multitask. Luckily for

him, he wasn't usually required to perform in all his capacities at once.

"Jenna's a miracle worker," Donna said. "That last engine job was hell on my hands, even with gloves on. And Perry likes my nails looking nice."

Once upon a time, pre-Good Riddance, Donna had been Don, star quarterback for his Midwestern college football team. Now Donna ran an engine repair shop across from the doctor's office. Gus thought it was touching Donna had found love with a prospector named Perry who didn't seem to mind a bit that Donna's parts were of the add-on variety.

"Your nails do look better, that's for sure," Jenna said to Donna, admiring her handiwork.

"Where's Curl?" Gus said.

Jenna wrinkled her nose. "He said he was skipping the hen party but actually he has a stuffing that has to be done for Henrietta Winters before Christmas."

Gus smiled at Jenna's "stuffing" terminology for Curl's taxidermy job.

"Okey dokey, that's got ya, Donna," Jenna said. "Why don't you switch places with Gus and give that a few minutes to dry and set before you head out?"

Donna stood. "I can't. I've got to get back 'cause Rusty's stopping by to talk about a carburetor problem we've got to get fixed before the snowmobile races, but I promise I'll be extra careful."

The door closed behind Donna and Jenna said, "You can go ahead and take off your boots and socks. Give me just a sec to reset my station."

"Just tell me when," Gus said.

She pulled off her shoes and socks, the air in Curl's cool against her bare feet. Maybe this time with Nick wouldn't be a bad thing. Keep your friends close, and your enemies closer. He wasn't exactly an enemy but... And as to the intense sexual attraction she'd felt for him, well, part of that had to be fueled by four years of abstinence coupled with the fact that once upon a time she'd been fairly infatuated with his writing. The odds were once she spent some time with him, she wouldn't like the reality of him nearly as much as she'd liked the man she'd created in her head through his work.

"When."

Gus snapped out of her reverie and looked at Jenna. "When what?"

"You said to tell you when, so come on over."

"Right." Gus slid into the seat across from Jenna who took Gus's hands in hers and frowned over what she saw. "Don't worry. We can fix this."

Gus obviously didn't know what she was looking at because she hadn't been worried in the least. She contented herself with saying, "Work your magic, Jenna."

Once Jenna had Gus's feet in the spa bath—which felt heavenly—she started on her hands. "Gus?"

"Yes?"

"I, uh, have a favor to ask?"

"What's that?"

"Do you think you could make up a special recipe for me?"

Gus hadn't known what to expect but it hadn't been *that*. "A recipe? What kind of food are we talking about?" Gus said cautiously. It was a bit of a strange conversation, well, even stranger than some conversations with Jenna could get.

"You know how those wolves marked Tessa?"

Tessa Bellingham had come to Good Riddance to record video footage. She'd hired Clint as her guide. Everyone knew interracial marriage was frowned upon by the natives in the area. But when wolves had "marked" Tessa by appearing before her three days in a row, she'd been accepted as a native and she and Clint were now engaged.

Gus had a bad feeling she knew where this was going. "Uh-huh."

"Well, I've been going out behind the cabin every day, hoping something would mark me." Jenna looked so sad Gus wanted to pat her shoulder in sympathy. "Nothing has. I need to be marked, so if you could come up with some kind of recipe I could put outside, ya know, to attract a wild animal so I'd be marked...." Jenna trailed off hopefully.

This definitely wasn't good. "Nelson?"

The other woman nodded, a mixture of adoration and despair reflected on her face. "I've never met anyone like him before. He's just so...so...cool and...sexy."

To borrow one of Merrilee's phrases, sweet mercy. In Gus's opinion Nelson was cool, but he'd never struck her as sexy. Regardless, he was one hundred percent barred from dating anyone outside his native heritage, marked or not. And Jenna, with her surgically enhanced breasts and blond-in-a-bottle, was obviously head over heels and equally obviously didn't stand a chance.

Gus laid it on the line. "You know he can't be involved with a white woman."

"That's why I want an animal to mark me, like it did Tessa." Jenna looked so hopeful, Gus simply couldn't bring herself to crush her.

"I'll see what I can come up with for you," she said, having absolutely no clue what else to do.

"Awesome." And just like that Jenna's train of thought jumped to another track. "Now let's give you some nice nails since you're going to have a hunky helper tonight."

Gus wasn't surprised Jenna knew. That was Good Riddance for you. There were no secrets here. Well, except for her secret...

And she fully meant to keep it that way.

4

CLINT WAS A NICE GUY, Nick thought as they drove down the snow-crusted road. So was his dog, Kobuk, sitting in the seat behind them, tongue lolling out as he looked out the window as if watching the evergreens lining the road. But then again, Nick had liked everyone he'd met so far, particularly the group he'd joined for dinner last night. They were all good people and intelligent with interesting stories. Of course, most people that wound up in out of the way places like Good Riddance had interesting stories.

"Spruce?" he hazarded a guess as to the evergreens.

"Yep. Right in one." Clint glanced briefly in Nick's direction. "So this is your first time in Alaska?"

"It is, if you can believe it." The tires seemed to crunch over the road. "Eight years of writing a travel blog and I've never been. It was long overdue."

Clint smiled his quiet smile. "Tessa enjoyed exchanging travel stories with you over dinner last night."

"Yeah, that was pretty cool we'd both been to Palenque." It was unusual to run into someone who'd visited the lesser-known Mayan ruins in Mexico's jungle. Nick shook his head. "And now she's going to give up all of that travel to stay here…. Sorry, I didn't mean that the way it came out." He couldn't quite wrap his head around it.

"No offense taken. I get what you're saying. I offered to move but she says her spirit belongs here."

Something moved at the edge of the trees and Nick thought he might've glimpsed a wolf, or perhaps it was just a malamute or husky. "The two of you have an interesting story, for sure. But then again, I figure most of the people who wind up here have an interesting tale to tell."

"For the most part. It takes a different kind to settle in Alaska, especially the bush."

And Nick was especially interested in one gray-eyed woman with a sensual mouth whom he couldn't seem to get out of his head. He aimed for casual. "So, what's Gus's story?" Damn, he was pathetic because merely saying her name aloud fired him up.

Clint laughed and sent him an amused glance. "I wondered how long it would take you to get around to asking."

So much for casual. "That obvious, huh?"

"Yes, pretty obvious."

"So?" This was close to pulling teeth and Nick had a sense Clint was testing him.

"She moved here—" he paused "—I guess it's been about four years now. Merrilee's her aunt. She was working in New York and apparently all the pressure got to her. She really kept to herself when she first got here."

"Her restaurant certainly seems to be part of the community fabric." It was funny, while she seemed friendly with everyone and her business was obviously central to the town, he'd noticed a guarded air about her, a slight distance.

"Gus's is practically an institution."

"Who had it before she took over?"

"A fellow named Hargood Winters ran it but it wasn't nearly as classy as it is now." That didn't surprise Nick in the least—Gus struck him as one classy woman. "Gus wound up buying him out and taking over."

Nick nodded in agreement but he knew better. She hadn't bought anyone out because her name wasn't part of the public records. He'd have to go back and look a little more closely because he was curious as to exactly who did own Gus's place.

"She's a hell of a chef," Nick said. "Some of the best food I ever had." Outside, a light snow began to fall.

"That's what everyone says. She was doing real well in New York—" Clint shrugged "—but apparently she just couldn't handle the pace."

"What restaurant did she work for?"

"I don't know but since I've never been to New York it wouldn't make any difference to me anyway."

Nick would bet that no one in Good Riddance could name the establishment she'd left. He didn't doubt she'd worked in the city, her culinary skills seemed that good, but he'd guarantee she wasn't known as Gus Tippens when she worked there.

"Does she still keep to herself?" Nick asked.

Clint offered a slow, knowing smile. "If you're asking

if she has a boyfriend, the answer is no. In fact, I've never known Gus to go on a date. Back when she first came into town, Dalton asked her out once or twice. She's not into hiking or fishing or camping so he offered to fly them into Anchorage for the evening since there's not a lot to do on a date in Good Riddance, except go hang out at Gus's."

Nick chuckled. "Yeah, I guess that's true. So, did she go out with him?"

"She was friendly, she was nice, but she turned him down."

Nick nodded. He'd seen firsthand how clearly besotted Dalton was with Skye Shanahan but he was still ridiculously relieved to know the other man had never kissed her or run his fingers through her hair. He had no right to feel proprietary about her in the least. Nonetheless, he did.

"And no, I don't think she's a lesbian," Clint added.

Nick startled and then laughed. "*That* never occurred to me."

They met an older Dodge pickup with a camper shell over the back and Clint raised a hand in greeting.

"You'll want to tread lightly there," Clint said, slanting him a glance. "Merrilee and Bull are pretty protective of her."

Nick quirked an eyebrow in question.

"I'm just saying. Maybe it's because she's Merrilee's niece or maybe it's because she was in pretty rough shape when she got here."

What the hell? All his journalist instincts, along with some protective male instinct that seldom surfaced, roared to life. He had a bad feeling deep in his gut. "What kind of rough shape?"

Clint glanced at him. Evidently his tension had come through in his question. "Emotionally. Mentally. You ever hear of something called alopecia?"

"No, I haven't. It doesn't sound good, though."

"It's when someone's hair starts to fall out or they start going bald. One of the triggers can be stress. That white streak in Gus's hair—that's where she had lost her hair and when it came back in, it came in white."

"Damn." He knew a culinary career in the city could be cutthroat but he'd seen Gus in the kitchen, albeit briefly, when she was swamped and she'd appeared competent and calm. She hadn't struck him as a woman who'd lose her hair and bury herself in the Alaskan backwoods due to performance anxiety. He was damn sure there was more to this.

"Yep. It wasn't good."

It struck Nick as a bit odd that Clint, a pretty quiet guy on the whole, was so forthcoming with information about Gus. Nick wasn't one to beat around the bush so he said exactly what was on his mind. "Why are you telling me all of this? You struck me as a pretty quiet guy."

Clint nodded. "I am, for the most part. But there's something you need to understand. In Good Riddance, we take care of our own. It's apparent you're interested in Gus. I just wanted to make it clear Gus has had a hard time in her life and none of us want to see a hard time come her way again."

Nick wasn't offended and didn't take it as a reflection

on his character. That's how he'd felt when his sisters were dating and even now that they were married—they'd better be treated right. He was glad Gus had people watching her back, whether she knew it or not. "Got it. Message received loud and clear."

He'd proceed with caution. The last thing he wanted to do was hurt Gus, but he did want her—he'd wanted her from the first glimpse he'd caught of her and each time he'd seen her since had intensified that feeling. And it wasn't just him indulging his male ego. Beneath that wariness in her gray eyes, he'd glimpsed a smoldering fire. He fully intended to fan those flames.

GUS HAD JUST FINISHED pulling the ingredients for the evening menu when Nick showed up that afternoon after the fireworks kicking off Chrismoose. She heard the door open but she *felt* him the moment he stepped into the room. It was as if she shared some strange cellular connection with this man.

"Reporting for duty, ma'am," he said from behind her, his voice low and smooth. She turned and his blue eyes met hers. Her breath seemed to lodge somewhere inside her chest as she recognized the flicker of desire in his eyes, which echoed her own. In a flash, she experienced the same tightening inside her she'd known last night and then again this morning. It was as if she were preparing for his touch and taste. One look and she was aroused.

Some dishes were best prepared by simmering, applying a low, constant heat over an extended period of time. Others required a hotter flame in a shorter span.

And then there was the technique of searing—brief, intense, extreme heat. The latter was what it was like to be around Nick Hudson—intense, scorching heat.

"There's an extra apron in the stock room if you'd like one," she said, pointing toward the door with her index finger.

"Probably a good idea," he said, moving across the room quickly. He moved with an economy of motion, which she liked, as if not to waste any effort. She also didn't miss noticing he had a very nice tush.

He donned the clean apron and once again turned his powerful blue gaze on her. "I'm at your disposal. Tell me what I can do for you," Nick said.

What he could do for her? She curled her fingers more tightly around the handle of the pot she'd just pulled out as she instantly imagined the whisper of his fingers through her hair, the taste of his kiss, the glide of his lips and tongue against hers, the press of his body, the melding of her heat with his. His eyes darkened and Gus could have sworn the same thoughts were running through his head, especially when his gaze dropped to her mouth. Without thinking, she ran her tongue over her lower lip and she felt tension radiate from him.

With a clang, she settled the pot on the stove, breaking whatever it was between them. She nodded toward the onions on the bottom shelf of the mobile cart she used to move things from one area to another.

"The onions need to be chopped, if you would."

His grin did funny things to her insides and it was knowing. He knew exactly what she was up to. "Sure thing. Onions are no problem. Minced, diced, or sliced?"

"Half diced and half sliced, if you would."

"If that's how you want it, that's how you'll get it. I aim to please."

She was burning up from the inside out and it wasn't the flu. "There's a lot to be said for intent, but the proof is in the pudding."

He leaned forward slightly over the work island separating them, his gaze dropping to her mouth, and she could swear just his look set her lips to tingling. "Then by all means, let me show you just how good I am—" there was a wicked pause accompanied by an equally wicked smile "—at slicing and dicing."

Gus laughed, despite feeling flustered and flushed. It was a good feeling to have this man she'd admired flirting with her. She should freeze him out. She should keep him at a distance. But she simply couldn't. He was slightly outrageous and she couldn't help but respond to him.

As much as she enjoyed her customers, she also enjoyed this time of the day. Lunch wrapped up at two-thirty, which was when Lucky called it a day. Gus came down at three and reopened at five-thirty for dinner. For two and a half hours it was just her and Teddy. Now it was just her and Nick.

It was odd how he seemed to fill out the space in her kitchen. Granted, he was a fairly big man, probably just a touch over six feet and broad shouldered, but it was more than that. There was a presence about him, an energy that seemed to expand into the area around him; that seemed to wrap around her.

Gus knew enough to realize Nick was definitely going to start asking questions if she didn't beat him to the punch. Plus, she was curious about him, especially after reading his columns.

She threw out a conversational gambit. "So, your parents have a diner in New York?"

"They did. They sold it last year. It's just a little place." He named a location she mentally mapped out in her head. She had a rough idea where it was. "But it's a good location. My grandparents had it and then the folks took over. I grew up there." He laughed and shrugged those impossibly wide shoulders. "Hey, it kept me off the streets."

While they each did their own thing, he regaled her with stories about his family and some of the incidents with different customers. Several times he had her laughing and she loved listening to the rhythm and cadence of his voice. She realized he was a natural storyteller.

"I get it now," she said, adding a bit more seasoning to the chicken stock.

"You get what?" He looked across the prep table that separated them. They were on simmer now. No searing, no flambéing, but definitely a simmer. This attraction, this thing was still there between them but laughter and the occasional companionable silence had dialed it back to a low heat.

"Why you're so good at what you do. You're a natural storyteller and I'm sure you never meet a stranger."

A quick smile curved his mouth and lit his eyes. He

acted as if she'd just handed him a blue ribbon. "You think I'm good at what I do?"

"Yes, you're very good at what you do. Of course, you don't need me telling you that because if you weren't, you wouldn't still be employed, would you?"

"True enough. I think it was the diner that set the stage for me. It was impossible to grow up there and not talk to people."

"You didn't catch the restaurateur bug?" He was definitely at ease in a kitchen. She'd wondered how she'd work with him distracting her, but it was just the opposite. She felt intensely tuned into everything she was doing.

He shook his dark head. "I like it and I certainly appreciate good food but my passion is the written word. My degree was in literature. It's not a particularly useful degree so I was damn lucky to get that internship and a job when I graduated."

"You travel all the time?"

"A fair amount. I'm gone at least a week out of every month."

"Doesn't that make it difficult to have any kind of stable life? A girlfriend or a pet? And that's not a criticism, just a question."

"True enough, I don't have any pets but I get home often enough to my folks. They've got the whole shmeal. Corky, a West Highland terrier, is the family dog. Gabbie is the cat who allows us to fawn over her. My mother has a cockatiel, Albert, more commonly known as Big Al because he never shuts up. My brother and two sisters and their families live within a block of my parents and my apartment's close by. My nieces and nephews have ferrets, hamsters, cats, dogs and fish. Trust me, it's a veritable zoo."

Wistfulness tugged at her. She'd always wanted to be part of a big family. Perhaps that was just the grass always being greener on the other side for an only child. And anyway, now in Good Riddance she had one huge extended family in the town itself. But that wasn't exactly what she'd been asking about. "You definitely have pets at your disposal, even if you don't own one yourself."

He grinned. "Were you trying to find out if I have a significant other?"

God he was brash and bold...and utterly charming.

"Maybe I was." Gus had almost forgotten how delicious it was to flirt with a man, even one who could give her away if he blogged about her.

"No significant other. A couple of years ago I had girlfriend and things were getting fairly serious and then she wanted me to quit my job. She didn't like the travel." He shrugged. "She told me it was the job or her and we see what decision I made. It was a good decision." Gus was most inappropriately relieved he didn't seem to still be carrying a torch for the woman from his past. "Any close calls on your part?"

Gus aimed for a casual shrug. She'd found sticking as close to the truth without giving too much detail sufficed. "I was engaged once. It didn't work out and that was a good decision, too." *That* qualified as the understatement of the year.

"Before you moved here?"

She turned back to the stove, away from the curiosity in his eyes. "Yes." She *would not* think about Troy now or that time.

He rounded the island to stand behind her, peering over her shoulder into the pot, inhaling. "Smells good." His shoulder lightly grazed hers and she quivered inside at the brief contact. "Well," he said, his breath stirring against her hair, "considering the ratio of men to women in Alaska, you can certainly pick and choose."

How was she supposed to think with him so close? Thank God, he took a step back. Her hand slightly unsteady, Gus dipped her spoon into the soup pot to taste test. She managed to cobble together a semi-coherent answer. "The problem with living in a town this size is that dating someone is a lot like dating someone at work. If things don't work out, then you still see them all the time and it can get really sticky."

She sipped at the spoon. Something wasn't quite right in the balance. She grabbed a clean spoon and handed it to Nick. "Tell me what you think."

"You really want my opinion?" He looked as if she'd just awarded him a prize.

"You seem to know your way around a kitchen."

He took the spoon from her and continued their conversation. "Then you know the solution to dating someone in town, don't you?"

"Enlighten me."

He tasted and paused. "Maybe a little more oregano?"

She nodded. That had been her take, as well.

Nick leaned against the prep counter, crossing his

arms over his chest, heart-thumpingly close. "If it's too sticky to date the locals, you find someone who's just passing through." His voice was low, soft and seductive, and his gaze seemed to devour her mouth. They'd gone from simmer to sear in about sixty seconds.

"I'll keep that in mind—" she paused deliberately "—if anyone passing through ever strikes my fancy."

5

NICK HAD THOROUGHLY ENJOYED himself. Merrilee had spent the evening waitressing while Nick had helped in the kitchen, and he and Bull had both worked the bar. Nick liked the mix of music, laughter and conversation all combined with the scents of good food. Even though he'd resented spending all of his summers and holidays working at his folks' diner, this reminded him it had also been damn good fun.

The whole place was buzzing with excitement over the late-afternoon fireworks, which had followed Merrilee's welcoming speech and kicked off the Chrismoose Festival and the upcoming competitions, and he'd met some real characters. It was just the kind of thing that offered the opportunity for him to gather great blog material—far better than if he'd just been sitting out at a table. Clint dropped by to tell him the pageant decorating committee could always use an extra pair of hands. Nick had said he'd be there. Working behind the scenes like that inevitably resulted in good info.

A little before ten, Gus walked over to the light switch

and flicked it off and on a couple of times. "Last call," she said to Nick with a smile. "It's better than yelling it."

Amazingly, within ten minutes the last customer had settled their bill and Gus locked the front door behind them. Nick watched Gus as she crossed the room. It had been a pleasure to watch her work in the kitchen. There was a passion and intensity to her when she was practicing her craft that he loved to see. It was as if behind a pot or pan, she lost that distance, that guardedness with which she seemed to surround herself. Gus unplugged.

Now a small frown creased her forehead when she looked at Merrilee.

"Thank you all for the help tonight. I couldn't have done it without you." Gus caught Bull's eye and gave him a look behind Merrilee's back that said *she's exhausted, take her home and put her to bed.* The older woman did look tired. Gus took Merrilee by the arm, heading toward the airstrip office door. "Goodnight, Bull and Merrilee, and thanks again," Gus said.

"But you've still got to clean up—"

Gus shook her head. "You helped last night. You look exhausted—"

"Thanks a bunch," Merrilee said.

"You're welcome because you do. Go." Gus stopped at the door and hugged the other woman. "Thank you for everything. You're a lifesaver."

"Are you sure—" Merrilee all but nodded in Nick's direction while he unabashedly watched the byplay. The two women were undeniably close although there wasn't a whit of family resemblance between the two of them.

"I'm sure. Say good night, Merrilee."

"Good night, Merrilee," she parroted.

Nick chuckled.

Merrilee added, "Good night, Nick." Her look, however, said *Buddy, you'd better watch yourself.*

"'Night," Bull said, giving Gus a nod that said he'd take over from here.

"Good night," Nick said.

The door closed behind her and Gus turned back to face him. Alone. Finally.

"Thanks again for your help tonight," she said. He had the impression she was thanking him again simply to have something to say now that it was just the two of them. He was glad she seemed as disconcerted by him as he was by her.

He walked back toward the kitchen. "I had a good time. Fill me in on your closing routine and I'll do Teddy's part."

"That's not necessary."

There was no way in hell he'd leave her to clean the entire place by herself. "I know it's not necessary but I don't do anything by half measures. If I'm filling in for Teddy, I'm doing what she'd normally do."

She glanced back at him over her shoulder as she pulled cleaning supplies out of a small closet, amusement lighting her gray eyes, the customary shadows he'd noticed there gone. "Do you always get your way?"

"Not always, but often enough."

"Often enough for what?"

"To get used to getting my way when it's something I really want."

And he wanted her.

SHAKING HER HEAD, she passed him a bucket, rag and disinfectant. "Fine then. You wipe down tables and stack the chair. I'll finish the kitchen and push the broom."

They worked quickly and efficiently, a comfortable silence settling between them. There remained however, a hum of awareness between both of them that was always there, that had been there from the beginning and that had gathered momentum throughout the night.

When they finished, Gus planted her hands on her hips and looked around as if amazed. "I have to say you're fast."

He crossed the room, letting her see the intent in his eyes, giving her the opportunity to retreat. "Sometimes you've got to move fast or an opportunity passes."

She stood her ground as he approached. "Is that a fact?"

"It is." He stopped in front of her, close enough to smell her scent, but not so close as to crowd her. He felt knotted up inside simply being this near her. "Now, I have a question for you. Since you're officially off work, would you like to go on a date with me?"

Her eyes widened slightly in surprise, accentuating the faint tilt at the corners. "Go on a date with you?"

"Sure. I've only got a couple of days here so I don't have any time to waste."

Her look was a mixture of wariness, amusement and banked heat. "What are we going to do on this date?"

"Get to know one another." He wanted to kiss her almost as much as he wanted his next breath, maybe more. "I happen to have the inside track on a great place in town that might run after hours. I was thinking a glass of wine and—" he nodded toward the silent jukebox "—maybe a dance or two."

She looked away, making it impossible to read her eyes. "And you were thinking when?" Her expression revealed very little. He had no idea whether she thought he was a total fool or not.

"Maybe half an hour. I'd like to change out of my work clothes."

A slow, sensual smile that sent his pulse into over-drive tilted the corners of her lovely mouth. "Forty-five minutes."

Hell, he'd wait an hour as long as it meant she'd show up. "Meet me at the bar?"

A sweet promise flickered in the depths of her eyes. "It's a date."

SHE'D LOST HER MIND. Obviously. Unequivocally. And she couldn't remember the last time she'd felt this alive and this energized. God knows, he was the last man she should want and God help her he was the only man she'd wanted in a long, long time.

Gus stripped out of her work clothes in double time and hopped in the shower. A date. She had a date. She laughed aloud at the sheer elegant lunacy of it. She had a date in her own restaurant after hours in the middle of the Alaskan bush with a man who had the potential to destroy everything she'd carefully built in the last four years. A man she'd barely known twenty-four hours. But Nick was no stranger to her. Spending time with him, working with him tonight… She was fairly certain he was the man she'd glimpsed in his writing.

Gus toweled off and dove under the counter in her bathroom. Somewhere…she had…where had she put it…had it gone bad…ah, there it was. She opened the perfume. Nope. It hadn't gone bad at all. She spritzed it behind her ears and, for good measure, down her cleavage. Making short work of the hair and makeup routine, she walked over to her closet.

Every day in Good Riddance was pretty much more of the same—dark slacks and the shirt du jour. But not tonight. She dug into the back of the closet, past the clothes that had served her well enough for the past four years. Yep, there it was, buried in the back, the quintessential little black dress. She hesitated, her hand on the hanger. The last time she'd worn it, she'd attended a function with Troy.

Squaring her shoulders, she determinedly pulled it off the hanger. She wouldn't let Troy keep her from wearing a dress she liked, just as she'd no longer let Troy keep her from going on a date. She tugged the black jersey and spandex over her head. It still fit like a glove. She turned and twisted in front of the mirror…actually, it fit better than it used to. She slipped on simple jewelry and a pair of low-heeled black shoes she hadn't worn since she'd worn the dress.

Downstairs the door creaked open between her place and the airstrip office. When the restaurant was open, with all the noise, you couldn't really hear it, but when it was quiet like this, there was no missing it.

She took one final look in the mirror, touched up her lipstick, drew a deep breath and stepped out into the hallway. She opened the door separating her apartment from the stairwell leading to the restaurant and bar. Her knees felt kind of shaky as she went down the stairs.

She stepped into the restaurant. Nick stood over by the bar. The lights were low, since she'd closed. In the corner, the lights twinkled on the Christmas tree that stood between the front door and the booths lining the wall overlooking Main Street.

He looked across the room and literally froze on the spot. "Oh...wow. You are breathtaking." There was no faking the note of awe in his voice.

Her heart, which was already racing, really went into overdrive. "Thank you. You don't clean up too badly yourself." He'd traded in his jeans and long-sleeved T-shirt for a pair of dress slacks and a button-down shirt.

He laughed, perhaps a tad self-consciously. "I learned a long time ago, you include one good outfit because you just never know what occasion might come up. So... maybe this is a little strange considering it's your place, but I was bartending earlier tonight and I'm serving you now. I've started a tab so what would you like? Oh, and where did you want to sit?"

It was all so wacky and kind of crazy and she loved it. "How about at the bar?"

"Perfect," he said. His look proclaimed he found her perfect, as well.

Her knees slightly unsteady, Gus slid onto the bar stool.

"And what type of libation can I serve you, mademoiselle?"

"I'll have a glass of the uncorked pinot noir."

"Coming right up."

He poured two glasses and joined her at the bar, slipping onto the stool next to hers. Part of her wished he'd left an empty stool between them, a little space. However, the rest of her was glad he was close. Although they weren't touching, she could almost feel his body heat, feel his energy mingling with hers. For a second his eyes caught and held hers and it was as if everything stilled. "Thank you," he said softly, all traces of his earlier banter gone, "for agreeing to come out with me tonight."

"I'm glad you asked." And she was, she realized. It was wonderful to feel this sense of anticipation, to feel like a woman.

His gaze searched hers. "Are you?"

It was pointless to pretend otherwise or play some coy game when he was only here for such a short time. "Yes."

He raised his glass. "To tonight."

"To tonight," she repeated, clinking her glass against his and then sipping. For Gus, that toast brimmed with significance. For tonight, she was putting the past firmly behind her, where it belonged. Tonight was about tonight.

"How about helping me deejay," he said. He stood. "Come on, let's pick out some music on the jukebox."

"Okay," she said, happy to go along with his suggestion. They stood in front of the jukebox, shoulder to shoulder. His scent, one of man, fresh soap and the faint scent of starch clinging to his shirt, was delicious. He braced one hand on the jukebox. She'd noticed his hands in the kitchen earlier—lean, well-shaped with long fingers and short, blunt nails. They went with the rest of him.

He fed a couple of dollars into the jukebox. "Okay, let's make some selections."

"Do you know how long this thing will play with that much money in there?"

"I'm hoping for a long date," he said, his voice teasing but his eyes serious. So was she. This was like a sweet, sweet dream she hadn't dared to dream. He scanned the playlist. "You've got quite a range of music here."

"Nelson's responsible for the selection. When he started as karaoke emcee, he put himself in charge of the jukebox content, which was fine with me." It was an eclectic range from Patsy Cline to Dean Martin.

Gus selected a Frank Sinatra number and Nick slanted her a glance. "You're a fan? He's one of my favorites."

"A boy from New York?"

His grin was straight-up boyish. "Absolutely."

They split the number of selections and went back to the bar, Nick guiding her lightly with his fingertips in the small of her back, which radiated heat throughout her. His touch proved as potent as she'd ever thought it might be.

Gus sipped at her wine and the conversation gravitated toward music. It turned out they shared similar musical tastes and had seen some of the same performers at New York venues.

One glass of wine turned into two and the conversation turned to books and movies and food and life in general. Gus found herself laughing and being laughed with. Nick seemed as entertained by her as she was by him and they had an astonishing amount in common. The things they didn't have in common remained a point of interest to Gus.

One of Gus's favorite Sinatra songs came up on the jukebox. Nick held out a hand. "Dance with me?"

She didn't hesitate. She didn't think twice. She put her hand in his. "I'd love to."

Maybe it was the man, perhaps it was the music, and two glasses of wine at the end of a long day probably didn't hurt, but Gus felt as if her feet weren't even touching the ground.

Held in his arms, against his warmth, his heart beating beneath her cheek, she seemed to float over the wood floor she'd trod uncountable times in the past four years.

The song ended and they stopped, standing still in the middle of the room. He leaned his forehead against hers, his warm breath gusting against her mouth. "Thank you for coming out with me tonight."

Her heart threatened to thump out of her chest. "I had a good time, Nick. I guess we should clean up, though. It's getting late."

He released her but kept her one hand in his and together they crossed to the bar. She washed up the glasses while he wiped down the counter, and then the crazy man insisted on settling his tab.

While they were cleaning up, the jukebox finished playing the final selection, leaving the room quiet once again.

She walked him to the door leading to the airstrip and B and B. He took her hands in his. "Come with me tomorrow. I'm helping decorate for the pageant."

She should say no. She meant to say no. Instead she said, "Okay."

"I can't remember when I've had more fun on a date," he said, bracketing her shoulders with his hands, his palms and fingers sizzling against her bare skin.

She barely bit back a sigh, looking up at him instead, and saying, "Me, too." She simply spoke the truth.

He released her and for one moment she thought he was going to walk through the door. Disappointment singed her but then he muttered, "Damn" as if he couldn't help himself. He caught her shoulders once again and his lips sought hers.

Gus met him halfway. Their kiss was warm, tender and he tasted like wine. He pulled her closer, kissing her deeper, more thoroughly and it was like a spark of lightning hitting underbrush at the end of a four-year drought.

Fire roared through her. Wrapping her arms around his waist, she moaned into his mouth. She absorbed his answering groan, as he proceeded to kiss her like she'd never been kissed before.

Finally he pulled away. Their mutually ragged breathing seemed to fill the room's quiet.

"If I'm going to leave, I need to leave now," he said, cutting to the chase.

He was clearly ready to stay if she issued the invitation. Gus wanted him, but for now it was enough to know he wanted her, too. And there was absolutely no doubt he wanted her. She released him. "I'll see you in the morning."

He turned loose of her arms and stepped back. "Good night, Gus."

"Good night, Nick."

He brushed his fingers over her cheekbone, as if driven to touch her just once more before he left. "Sweet dreams."

For the first time in a long time, she thought she just might. "You, too."

He stepped through the door and she closed it behind him. Sighing, she leaned against it and smiled, simply because she couldn't do otherwise. Her lips were still warm from his, his taste still lingered against her tongue.

Hands down, it was, quite simply, the most romantic date she'd ever experienced.

"MERRILEE, YOU NEED TO STAY out of it," Bull said from behind the hardware counter in his store.

Merrilee, who'd hardly slept a wink all night despite being exhausted, had headed over to see him as soon as she'd put the coffee on at the office and Jeb and Dwight had shown up.

Bull simply didn't understand the workings of a

woman. Although he seemed to muddle along well enough at times, he didn't get it now.

Merrilee cocked one hand on her hip and stared him down. "Are you hearing what I'm telling you? He was over there until after 2:00 a.m. this morning. You know she closes the place at ten. He came over to the B and B, showered, and then went back over there and didn't drag in until two."

Unperturbed by her outburst, Bull casually picked up a piece of wood and pulled out his knife. "Gus is a grown woman and God knows she's lived like a damn nun since she moved here."

"But *him?*" Was Merrilee the only one who had any sense when it came to Nick? He was like a snake-oil salesman who'd cast a spell over everyone he'd met, except her. "What is Gus thinking?"

Wood shavings flew from the edge of the knife as Bull whittled. "She's probably thinking she's long overdue some time with a man. Leave the girl alone."

He didn't get it. "She's my responsibility."

"No. She came here a mess and we helped her. She's not your responsibility. She's a grown woman who can make her own decisions. The same way Jenna made her decision about Tad." He rocked his chair back on two legs and propped his feet up on the shelf beneath the counter. "You've got to get over this sudden urge to save all the twentysomethings from what you see as mistakes. You can't go back and undo your past by interfering in theirs."

They'd had arguments before but for the first time in the twenty-five years she'd known Bull Swenson, she was furious with him. Anger rolled through her like a firestorm.

She rounded on him. "Am I just supposed to stand by while they make these mistakes?" His relaxed posture when she was so upset further annoyed the hell out of her.

"Yes, you are."

"But…."

"Merrilee, honey, as much as you want to take care of everyone and protect everyone, you can't. You have to allow people to follow their own paths."

"And what if you know they're making a big mistake?"

"That's life and the freedom to live it. Baby, you've made big mistakes and it wasn't as long ago as twenty-five years."

Ouch. She guessed he'd been waiting for that. Apparently Bull wasn't as perfect as she'd thought and didn't quite fight fair when backed in a corner.

Merrilee raised her chin. "Yes, I have made some mistakes. I should've told you I wasn't divorced from the beginning and I didn't. To your point, I can't undo the past, so when are you going to forgive me for that?"

"I've forgiven you, Merrilee." He put the chair down on all four legs and stood, suddenly looking as weary as she felt. "I just can't seem to forget."

She'd hurt him and that was the last thing she'd ever wanted to do to this man, but she couldn't change the past. If she could, she would—in a heartbeat. "Well, maybe it's not so much a matter of forgetting as it is letting go."

"I'm trying. It's as if we lived a lie for twenty-five years." He rubbed at his shoulder and she knew his old war wounds were giving him a fit. But it didn't change the fact he was wrong.

"No. We didn't live a lie for twenty-five years. What was…is…between us is real. That's always been real—there's no lie there." She raised her chin a notch and stared into his sherry-brown eyes. "I've been in love with you from the moment I first laid eyes on you, Bull Swenson."

"Then dammit, woman, when are you going to make an honest man of me?" Bull didn't get upset often, but he was upset now. She could tell by the stiff set of his shoulders and the impatient edge in his voice.

For all his gruff manner, Marine tattoos, and the long gray hair he kept pulled back in a ponytail, Bull was surprisingly conventional. He'd been asking her to marry him on a regular basis since she'd first met him. Then when he'd found out she and Tad were still married, Bull had told her he wouldn't be asking her to marry him again. Next time, he'd implied the asking would be up to her. He was handing her the opportunity now. And she simply couldn't.

For all her traditional Southern upbringing, she wasn't nearly as conventional as Bull. Plus, she'd spent thirty-seven years legally tied to a man she didn't want to be legally tied to. Albeit the last twenty-five years she and Tad had been apart, but she'd been legally bound to him nonetheless. Why in the world would she want to step back into that mess all over again? From her perspective it was way too easy to get married and far too hard to get unmarried.

"I guess I don't see the point, Bull. Does a piece of paper mean I love you more? No. It's not as if we have children together."

His eyes seemed to bore straight through to her soul. "It means commitment."

Had she missed something? Apparently she had. "I don't know how either one of us can be any more committed than we have been. I haven't looked at another man and I know you haven't looked at another woman. We've taken care of one another when we were sick, we've seen each other through lean times. We've lived those vows you take in a church, so what difference does it make?"

"It means I get to call you my wife."

Merrilee had no answer for that.

6

NICK CAME DOWNSTAIRS and headed for the restaurant, nodding a greeting to the two old-timers over at the chess table. Merrilee wasn't at her desk and he was just as happy to escape her sharp-eyed censorship this morning.

He was a hundred percent sure she'd heard his comings and goings last night. He also was pretty damn sure she wouldn't approve. He got a vibe from her and he didn't know if it was fear, wariness, distrust, or general dislike. Hell, it might even be a combination thereof—he wasn't on her favorite person list and he'd be damned if he knew why. Most people liked him.

His gut told him it had something to do with Gus. Merrilee hadn't wanted to leave him alone with Gus in the restaurant last night. There was her whole general protectiveness, but his instincts told him there was more to it. He was certain it had something to do with the mystery of Gus's true identity and her exodus from New York.

He'd lain awake last night, well, technically this

morning, turning everything over in his head. He couldn't remember when he'd had as good a time as he had last night—all parts of the evening from working in the restaurant to his date with Gus, although his date with Gus definitely ranked highest, and that kiss...

The woman did something to him. He'd always been very discriminating about his lovers. Not only was it prudent, but it was just the way he was made. But last night he would've climbed right into bed with her, something he'd never done on a first date, if she'd just given him the word.

In turning things over in his head, something kept niggling at the back of his brain, but it wouldn't fall into place. He shrugged. What he needed would come to him if he was just patient. He could practically hear his mother reassuring him as she had so many times in the past when he was impatient with life, *in good time, Nicky, in good time.*

He walked through the connecting door, the aroma of eggs, bacon and fresh coffee beckoning. Clint and Dalton sat at the bar, nursing cups of java. Nick glanced around, looking for Gus, but didn't spot her.

"Hey, Nick. Hunting some breakfast?" Clint said.

Dalton looked at Clint and grinned. "Nah, he's hunting for Gus." Dalton looked back at Nick. "She hasn't come down yet this morning. Apparently she had a pretty late evening last night."

Well, so much for being subtle in looking around for Gus. While there were obviously some secrets floating around in Good Riddance, for the most part it seemed everyone's business was public. It was eight-fifteen in the a.m. and already their late night was common knowledge. Nick had a new appreciation for Gus's explanation of why dating in Good Riddance could be very awkward.

He simply smiled and slid into the empty stool next to Clint. "Breakfast sounds good."

"By the way," Clint said, "I told my cousin you'd volunteered to help decorate for the pageant. She said around twelve-thirty."

"I'll be there," Nick said. And so would Gus, but he didn't volunteer that information. He bit back a grin. There was no need given the way news traveled here. Luckily, he found it part of the town's charm.

Mavis, a tall raw-boned woman, who covered the breakfast and lunch shift, poured Nick a cup of coffee and took their orders. The front door opened and a short, squat woman, her black hair plaited in a single braid down her back, entered. "Hey, Clint, Dalton," she said by way of greeting.

"Speak of the devil," Clint said. He introduced the woman as his and Nelson's cousin, Luellen Sisnuket. "Nice to meet you," she said. She had the same melodic cadence as Clint and Nelson.

Mavis wandered over. "What's up, Luellen?"

The shorter woman looked positively mournful. "Trouble in paradise. That's what."

"What do you mean?"

"They're dropping like flies. Nelson called me a few minutes ago. Curl has the flu."

It occurred to Nick that were they anywhere else, it would be a huge breach of patient confidentiality for one of the medical staff, namely Nelson in this case, to call up someone other than the patient and discuss a diagnosis, but Good Riddance seemed to rock along to a rhythm all its own.

He didn't have to turn his head to know Gus had entered the room and walked over. He recognized her scent and it was as if he possessed a sixth sense when it came to her. He looked to his left. Sure enough, she was approaching the counter looking pulled together in a black sweater over black pants, silver earrings and her signature red lipstick. For a second their eyes met and it was as if something special passed between them. A radiant smile lit her face and he grinned back like a fool.

When he turned back to the group, Dalton tugged at the collar of his shirt. "It sure got hot in here all of sudden," he said with a teasing smirk. "Do you think it's hot, Clint?"

Clint nodded, a gleam in his eyes. "Definitely."

Smart-asses. Mavis, the true meaning of the exchange going straight over her head, peered at both Dalton and Clint in concern. "I sure hope you two aren't getting sick, 'cause it don't feel any different in here to me."

"We'll be alright," Dalton said.

"Morning," Gus said by way of general greeting. "So, Curl has the flu now?" Apparently she'd caught the last part of Luellen's announcement and being the wise woman she was chose to ignore Dalton and Clint's sly ribbing.

Luellen nodded. "Yeah, so now we're short a judge for the Ms. Chrismoose pageant tomorrow night."

Mavis glanced from Dalton to Clint, a speculative gleam in her eye. "Since both of you are feeling okay...."

"Nope," Clint said.

Dalton shook his head and threw up a hand. "No way."

Both men looked at Nick. It was Dalton who offered the explanation. "It's hell to live in a town and be a pageant judge. Three contestants wouldn't speak to me for nearly six months afterwards the one year I was dumb enough to get rooked into it."

Mavis was looking at Nick. "Would you—"

What the hell? He didn't live here, nor did he plan to. It'd be fun. "I could—" Nick spoke at the same time.

"Would you, really?" Mavis beamed.

"I think it'd be cool," Nick said. "I've never been a pageant judge before."

Dalton snorted and gave him a pitying look. "That's what I thought, too, man." He grinned. "Of course, you don't have to live here afterwards either so it'll probably work out okay for you."

Luellen nodded, a faint smile curving her mouth. "That's a big relief."

"Luellen and I head up the pageant committee," Mavis explained to Nick. "You just took a big headache off our plate. Thank you."

It was a totally mixed metaphor but he knew what she meant.

At his elbow, Gus laughed. "You're quite the volunteer. Better watch out or when it's time for you to leave, the town might not let you go."

Luellen gave another one of her solemn nods. "Good Riddance has a way of doing that. We captivate people and then they don't want to leave."

Dalton nodded. "Skye warned you the other night. Sometimes this place just gets in your blood."

Nick laughed but he wanted to make sure Gus was clear on who and what he was. "As charming as I find your town, I'm the traveling man. My job takes me all over the world and then back to New York."

Gus seemed to be suddenly busy with something over by the register and didn't look up. But he had no doubt she'd heard him.

Luellen sagely intoned, "We'll see."

"Mavis, these eggs are getting cold," Lucky yelled from the kitchen.

Tapping on the counter, Mavis said, "Hold on boys, let me snag your eats."

Gus finished up whatever she'd been doing over by the register and poured a cup of coffee. She hefted the pot in their direction. "Anybody need a refill or topping off?"

"Nah, I'm good," Clint said while Dalton shook his head no.

"I'll take a little more," Nick said. What he'd take was another kiss given half an opportunity but it certainly wouldn't be here and now.

"Gus is our reigning Ms. Chrismoose," Mavis said, returning with their plates. "She'll have to give up her crown tomorrow night."

Well, damn. He'd been looking forward to seeing her

as a contestant. Pageants always included a swimsuit competition, didn't they?

A faint blush crawled up her face. Nick couldn't help but tease her. "I didn't know I was dealing with a crowned queen."

"You're kidding," Dalton said with a smirk. "She's had us all bowing and scraping for the past year."

"*You* need to bow and scrape right now, Saunders," Gus said, narrowing her eyes in mock annoyance.

Dalton grinned while Nick and Clint laughed. Nick could see how a person could get easily get caught up in this little town. But that was neither here nor there for him. He was out of here in a couple of days and on to the next assignment.

GUS LIKED THE WAY NICK HELD the door for her as they left the restaurant that afternoon to go to the community center. But then again, she was hard-pressed to find something she didn't like about this man. Even though the streets were bustling with the influx of adults, kids and animals for Chrismoose, now that they weren't part of a group Gus suddenly felt self-conscious with Nick.

All she'd been able to think about this morning in the restaurant was the taste, the texture, the heat of his mouth against hers and how much she wanted to feel that again, and more, much more. And how it was damn near impossible to find a private moment when you lived in a teeny tiny town where your business was everyone else's business.

She shot a sidelong glance at his mouth, the lines of his face etched into her brain. He was handsome in a way that stole her breath. It wasn't simply the slant of his nose or the angle of his cheekbones or those piercing blue eyes that made him breathtaking. It was the man beneath who displayed wit and insight, who painted a picture with words that brought a place to life, a man who embraced each experience with enthusiasm, curiosity and appreciation. A man who had danced her across the floor of her closed restaurant and then kissed her into a new dimension. All told, she really didn't think she could wait until tonight to kiss him again. But given the throngs of people, she might as well redirect her thoughts to more realistic matters.

"We'll have to walk," Gus said. "I don't have a car."

"No problem." Nick grinned and turned up the collar of his coat. "Spoken like a true transplanted New Yorker. I don't have a car either. Traffic is ridiculous and it's too expensive to garage it."

Gus knew exactly what he meant. "Yep. I either cabbed it, walked, or took the subway when I lived there. I just walk now." There was a lot of traffic out this morning. Two trucks and a rusted out car had already passed them.

"Is there even a cab that runs here?" He didn't sound critical, simply curious. That was yet another thing she liked about him—his curiosity, even though it could be her own downfall, except he couldn't possibly discover her real name. She admired how interested he was in everything. Perhaps it was his appreciation for all the minutia of life that made his blog so interesting.

She grinned. "Not like a yellow checkered cab.

There's Perry, who prospects a couple of miles out of town. If someone needs a ride, he's the go-to guy. That's how he and Donna met, when she fixed his gear box."

He glanced down at her. "Does everyone here have a story?"

Before she could reply, he reached between them and took her gloved hand in his. The two of them walking down the sidewalk holding hands would be all over town before they even reached the community center, but Gus didn't care. She left her hand in his and answered his question.

"Pretty much."

She could feel it pulsing between them, his curiosity as to her story. It was inevitable he'd ask prying questions. She jumped in with one of her own first. "What'd you think of the ice fishing?"

He'd hitched a ride after breakfast with Clint and Dalton out to where the tournament was being held.

"It was interesting. A couple of guys were still setting up so it was cool to watch them auger a hole through the ice and get settled. There were almost as many women out fishing as men, plus a handful of kids. I thought that was great. I'm certain I wouldn't have the patience to just sit there on the ice all day, though."

"You and me both."

He grinned down at her and her heart seemed to somersault in her chest. "You're not a fishing enthusiast?"

"Hardly."

"I love the moose along the street," Nick said, changing the subject.

"They're fun, aren't they? The kids all love them."

The air was crisp without being biting cold, and snow drifted down as if it couldn't quite decide whether to fall or not. For whatever reason the day seemed brighter than usual.

"How long did it take you to get used to the long hours of dark in the winter?" Nick asked. The sun had finally broken December's seemingly interminable darkness, but it would be a brief appearance.

Gus shook her head. "Don't tell anyone but I'm still not used to it." She hated the long days of dark. She didn't think she'd ever make the adjustment.

"Do you miss New York?"

She didn't answer right away, weighing it, trying to be honest with herself. "There are things about it I miss," she said slowly, a bit of a melancholy drifting over her. She'd tried to block it from her mind for the past several years since it was no longer an option, but the conversation with Nick forced her to acknowledge it. "Christmas in New York is incomparable. Rockefeller Center, the department store decorations, the crowds, the Santas working the corners, Central Park."

"I know. There really isn't anything like it anywhere else, is there?" He sent another of his casual glances her way which didn't feel casual at all. It felt more as if he were peering into her very soul, regardless of whether she wanted him there or not. "Have you been back to the city since you moved here?"

She made a concerted effort not to tense. "No. I haven't been back."

"You should plan a trip around Christmas."

She laughed and she knew it sounded a bit forced.

"It's not that easy to just take a trip when you own your own business, especially a restaurant. You should know that with your parents' place."

"Yeah, true enough."

They passed the medical center. The waiting room was packed. Even the unflappable Nelson appeared harried behind the mask he wore. Gus waved and Nelson returned the greeting.

"If Nelson and Skye get sick, everyone's out of luck," Gus said, eager to talk about something other than New York.

"How close is the next nearest doctor?"

"You don't want to know."

It was funny. When Gus had met both Skye and Tessa, she'd known both of them belonged in Good Riddance. Nick also fit in beautifully. Everyone liked him and he fully embraced all aspects of their little community, but even before he'd made it clear this morning, Gus had known with equal certainty he didn't belong here. He'd never stay.

And she didn't know if that was a good thing or a bad thing.

A COUPLE HOURS LATER, as they wrapped up the last of the decorating in the community center, Nick thought it very likely he was losing his mind. He'd never had a woman affect him this way. It was as if he couldn't get enough of Gus. On every level he'd been aware of her the entire time. It was as if he was consumed with the need to kiss her, touch her. And meanwhile it was as if they were on public display. As much as he liked

Good Riddance, there was precious little privacy to be found here.

"Can you drape that garland a little more to the left?" Luellen asked.

Nick shifted on the ladder and redraped the greenery per her request. Meanwhile Gus arranged spruce boughs at the judges' table. Clint had delivered folding chairs from Curl's, Tessa's new screening room/video rental place, and the nondenominational church that anchored the other end of Main Street.

"Looks great," Luellen said.

Nick nodded and climbed down the ladder. The room did look pretty good. It was evident everyone was proud of their new facility. According to Clint, the final touches had only been finished yesterday.

"Anything else?" he asked.

Luellen looked around, her mouth pursed in assessment. "I think that's it. Gloria's going to finish up the papier-mâché around the stage and that's it."

Gus checked her watch, a no-nonsense utilitarian affair. "If that's it, I need to be getting back. Lucky and Mavis should be almost done with the lunch crowd and I wanted to make a pot of chicken soup for Teddy and a pot for Curl."

"We're done here. Thanks for your help," Luellen said. Shifting her weight to her other foot she continued, "That's really nice of you to do that for Curl, especially since he lives alone." She looked at the floor. "I could take it over for you once you get it made...if you wanted me to since you'll probably be busy."

"Sure." Gus smiled at Luellen. Every time she smiled,

it sent a little rush of heat through him, even when her smile wasn't directed at him. "That would actually be a big help. I'll give you a call when it's ready."

Gus and Nick retrieved their coats and bundled up. They stepped out into the cold. The sun was close to exiting on the horizon. Once they were out of hearing distance of the community center, Gus shook her head. "It must be cabin fever."

She'd lost him. "Cabin fever?"

A barking dog ran past them, a boy of about six in pursuit, calling out, "Ringo, wait for me."

"Yeah. First there's Jenna crushing on Nelson. And now Luellen obviously has a thing for Curl. It seems to happen about this time every year. I think it's cabin fever."

"You're serious? This is really a phenomenon?" It would explain much of his reaction to Gus. Granted, he hadn't been in winter lockdown mode like the rest of the town, but still...

"I'm serious as a heart attack. I noticed the same thing last year."

"Well, it must be catching."

"How's that?"

He caught her hand in his again. He liked holding it. He'd like to kiss her as well, but for now her hand in his was better than nothing. "Will you go out with me again tonight?"

Her smile gave him all the answer he needed. "Where are we going this time?"

Yes. The day seemed to get a little brighter despite the impending sunset. "Once again, I have a connection.

How do you feel about shooting pool and throwing darts?"

They dodged a mound of snow on the sidewalk. "I'm not very good at either one."

He laughed. "Don't tell anyone, but neither am I. It's really just a ruse to get you to say you'll go out with me again."

She arched one eyebrow. "So we can play bad pool together?"

"Pretty much so I can spend time with you. Should I pick you up after work?"

"How about I just meet you there?"

He liked how she went along with the ridiculousness of meeting at her place after hours as a date. "That works. When we get back I've got to some things to do and I want to check out a couple of the artists, but then I'll be over to work as your galley slave again." Each business in town was hosting two or three artists in their location. It spread traffic out and got people into the local shops.

She laughed. "You really don't have to help out. I appreciate it but I'm sure you didn't come here to sub in a restaurant."

"That's the beauty of what I do. I can do whatever pleases me as long as I can pull an article out of it. And it pleases me to help you in your restaurant. I just need to make a few notes, write my post and send it."

Once again, because he was used to studying people and watching their expressions, he saw the flash of apprehension that momentarily shadowed her eyes and tensed her jaw.

He stopped right there on the sidewalk, and turned her to face him. "Gus, I don't know who or what you're running or hiding from but you asked me not to blog about you or your establishment and I won't."

Acceptance and a measure of trust were in her eyes, but there was also still darkness. He could almost feel the tension inside her. "Thank you."

They resumed their stroll down Main Street. He wouldn't blog about her or her business, but that didn't mean he wouldn't keep digging until he uncovered the secret that put those shadows in her eyes.

7

NICK WALKED INTO THE AIRSTRIP center an hour later, having stopped by every business to check out the artists and their crafts. The airstrip office was hopping, as well. Merrilee had set up a landscape painter in the front, a beader in the middle of the room and a flute carver over near the bank of windows overlooking the landing strip out back. The hum of conversation along with the aroma of coffee, cookies and wood smoke hung in the air.

Merrilee was busy talking with the wood-carver and the three or four people. She wore a smile but there was no mistaking the dark circles beneath her eyes. He knew with a surety his time with Gus last night had put them there.

Grabbing a cup of coffee and snagging a couple of cookies—chocolate chips were his favorites—he headed upstairs to his room. He'd check out the artists later, on his way to the restaurant. Right now, he was eager to get his thoughts down.

Settled in his room, he made notes on his laptop, wrote his latest post, and made short work of the coffee and cookies. Nick set his computer to the side and leaned back against the headboard. Grabbing a pen and notepad, he began to make a list of what he knew about Gus and her situation.

Left New York four years ago. Changed her name. Didn't travel now. Did not want her business in his blog. Merrilee's friendliness up until she found out Nick's occupation. Restaurant wasn't in Gus's name. No public records on her at all. The shock of white in her hair a result of extreme stress. Merrilee extremely protective. Gus, friendly but holding herself apart from the rest of the town. Shadows in her eyes.

He closed his eyes and thought. There had been something yesterday and then today. Something that struck him as similar chords. Got it. He opened his eyes. It was the look on her face when he'd asked her if she'd ever had a close call and she said she'd been engaged. It was the same expression she'd assumed when he'd asked her today if she'd ever returned to New York. Both questions had elicited a neutral expression and sometimes that could be as revealing as wearing your emotions on your face. It meant she was carefully hiding her true response to both of those questions.

He began to doodle on the page and draw arrows from one part of the list to the other. He stopped and read through his notes one more time.

He reorganized his notes, listing them in as close to chronological order as possible. A picture emerged. It was pure deduction on his part, but that's what solved cases and mysteries.

Putting all the parts together, his best guess was Gus

had an engagement that had gone bad. He'd speculated she was running from someone and that was her ex-fiancé. It would explain the name change, the not dating anyone for the last four years, and the general protective-ness surrounding her.

And the way he saw it that fiancé was still in New York. Merrilee's demeanor had changed when she'd found out he wrote for the *Times*. Gus had point-blank asked him not to mention her, which told him if he did, this man could then find her. It also told Nick if she'd gone to those measures, this man was dangerous in the extreme.

If he was right, and his gut told him he was, he was even more determined to solve this and do something about this guy. And now, there was an equal measure of desperation gnawing at him. The thought of anyone threatening Gus made his blood run cold with a fury he hadn't known he possessed.

If she would just trust him, and he knew that wasn't something that would come easily, he could help her. Without a name, hers or her former fiancé's, Nick's hands were tied.

IMPATIENCE RACKED HER. Gus had always taken great pleasure in preparing food and having people enjoy it, in the scents and sounds of running a restaurant. Tonight, however, she simply wanted everyone to finish clearing out so she could have her date with Nick.

And she was dead certain Nick had the same idea. More than once tonight he'd sent a smoldering glance her way. She'd smoldered right back at him. Her body had felt too tight for her skin all afternoon. She'd obviously caught the cabin fever, too.

"Psst, Gus, hey."

Jenna, at the edge of the pickup counter, waved Gus over. "Hey, have you had any luck in coming up with... well, what we talked about the other day, ya know, *the recipe?*"

Oops. Guilt pinged her. She'd been so wrapped up in Nick, in herself, she'd forgotten all about Jenna's recipe request.

Gus had no idea what the heck she was going to pull together for Jenna, but she'd come up with something. "I promise I'll get something to you tomorrow. How's Curl?"

As with Gus and some of the other business owners, Curl lived above his business. It was much more efficient to build up than build both a business establishment and a separate residence.

"He was better when I left this afternoon. Luellen brought by your soup. She stayed with him for a long time." She dropped her voice to a conspiratorial whisper. "I think she might like him. Just give me a call when you've got it ready. I'm pretty booked tomorrow because of the pageant, but I'll find time to run over and pick it up. I'm desperate. You-know-who doesn't seem to know I'm alive."

Gus felt terrible for Jenna. This situation had heartache written all over it. But she just couldn't bring herself to crush the other woman's hopes. "I'll see what I can do, Jenna."

"Thanks, Gus. You're the best, right behind Merrilee."

Funny how Merrilee and Jenna had become close when the only things they really had in common was they were women and they'd both had the bad taste to get involved with Tad Weatherspoon but the good sense to dump him.

"I'll call you tomorrow," Gus said.

Jenna drifted into the dining room and Gus got back to work. Finally, she locked the door behind her last customers and turned around. Even though Merrilee had protested, Gus had refused her help this evening. Between Chrismoose and the stress of the situation with Nick, Merrilee had clearly been exhausted. Bull had helped with the bar until around nine when Gus had insisted he check on Merrilee.

She and Nick had been busy the last hour, but it had been manageable. Now Nick stood in the kitchen opening. "You know, I spend more time alone in a city of thousands than I do in your town of hundreds," he said with a smile.

Gus nodded. "And especially here in the restaurant and bar where there's always someone around from six until ten."

"Trust me, I've figured that out." He lowered his voice and his look sent a shiver of anticipation down her spine. "Come here, Gus."

She crossed the room on unsteady legs, her heart thumping in her chest like a mad thing. She stopped in front of him. "Yes? You wanted something?"

He bracketed her face in his hands. "Yeah. This. All day."

Nick slowly lowered his head and feathered his

lips over hers. She sighed and linked her arms around his neck, holding on. It was nice, but it wasn't nearly enough. She wanted more. Gus pressed her lips more firmly against his and turned it into a real kiss.

Oh, oh, oh. His mouth was heaven against hers. It felt as if it had been an eternity rather than a mere day. She buried her fingers in his hair and relished the feel of his body against hers. It faintly registered in the back of her mind that the last time a man had been pressed against her it had been menacing. She pushed the thought aside and gave herself over to the here-and-now experience of kissing Nick in her kitchen.

He deepened the kiss yet even further, his tongue seeking entry to her mouth. She opened herself to him. He tasted faintly of curry—from one of her dishes he'd sampled tonight—and he smelled deliciously like man and aftershave, or maybe it was deodorant. Who knew? She just knew she liked it a lot—his feel, his heat, his cent, his taste, and most definitely his touch.

They finally broke apart, coming up for air and a bit of reality settled in for her. "We have to do the nightly cleaning." Her voice was definitely unsteady.

"I know." His breath was as ragged as hers. "How about we make it quick? I've got a date tonight."

She laughed. "Good help is so hard to find."

"Woman... Let's get this done."

He was a man with a mission, and truth be told, she had the same mission. They cleaned the place in record time.

Nick paused at the door to the B and B. "Back here in half an hour?"

Gus laughed at how flatteringly eager he was for their date. She was, too, but she needed more than half an hour for hair and makeup. "Forty-five minutes."

"I'll be here."

"See you then," she said, crossing to the door to her private quarters upstairs. She felt him watching her.

Gus opened the door and stepped into the stairwell, closing the door behind her. She leaned back against the wood panel. What was it about Nick that she felt this connection? It had zapped her from the first moment she saw him—in reality, far before she'd ever actually met him. Was it that he pitched in without complaint regardless of what needed to be done? Was it his tales of travel? The way he listened when she spoke, as if he really wanted to know what she had to say?

Perhaps he represented the New York she'd loved but left behind. Maybe he was the rest of the world to her small corner in Good Riddance. Could it be because from the moment she'd laid eyes on him, her sexuality, dead for the last four years, had been resurrected?

Gus really didn't know for sure. Maybe it was all of the above. The one thing she knew for absolutely certain was while he was here, she wanted Nick Hudson and she meant to have him.

NICK MADE IT BACK OVER to the restaurant in record time. He knew he'd be ahead of Gus but that was fine. He poured each of them a drink, before killing the lights in the bar, the kitchen, and the front two-thirds of the restaurant. The Christmas tree lights twinkled merrily in the dark. Placing their glasses on the table, he racked the balls on the pool table. It was odd how everyday mundane things took on a fun quality with her.

She had a ready smile and a friendly word for each of her customers and he got the impression it wasn't simply because they were customers. But beneath it all was a wariness, a reserve. He'd spent enough time around people to recognize a woman with major trust issues when he met her. Gus held everyone at an arm's distance, except for Merrilee which was no surprise considering they were family.

He crossed to the jukebox and selected some of the same music they'd both enjoyed last night. They had similar taste in music. Actually, they seemed to have quite a bit in common.

He was so sure he'd figured out what was going on with her, or he was at least damn close. Whenever they spoke about New York she lit up. She was interested in the places he'd traveled. She didn't belong here. She got along well enough with everyone but it wasn't as if she fit here the way the other citizens did.

He heard her footfall on the stairs and turned, waiting. His breath literally caught in his throat when she opened the door, a smile curving her lips. Her dark hair framed her face. That white streak always gave her a striking look along with the almond shape of her eyes. She'd pulled on a black top that hugged her curves in all the right places, jeans and silver hoop earrings.

"You look lovely," he said. For a man who made his living with words, that seemed terribly inadequate.

"Thank you. You clean up pretty nicely yourself." He'd also opted for jeans, and a long-sleeved polo shirt.

She moved into the bar, closing the door behind her. "So, are you ready to see which of us is worse at this game?"

He laughed. "I know any self-respecting man should be ashamed to admit it but I'm pretty bad." He indicated the glasses on the table near the pool table. "A drink before we start?"

"It sounds good to me. Actually, it can only improve my game."

"I hear you on that."

He held her chair for her and then joined her at the table. Her knee brushed against his and awareness arrowed through him. Their eyes met and the memory of their kisses was there between them, but by unspoken agreement they decided not to rush. They'd get there.

"Clint said you took over the restaurant from someone else?" Nick had done a public records search earlier and learned Bull Swenson owned the building and held the business license for Gus's.

"I took it over and then I expanded some. Good Riddance's population had grown a good bit since the original building was built about fifteen years ago. It was always packed in here and I was pretty sure I could draw an even bigger crowd." She smiled and pointed to an area near the third table out. "That's where it used to end. The living quarters were pretty tight so we expanded the second floor, as well."

"My place in New York is small. I figure why put out a lot of bucks for a bigger space when I'm there so seldom." Nick glanced around the room. "If it's the same size as down here, you've got a big place up there." And hell, yeah, he was angling. He wanted to see where she lived, where she relaxed. He wanted a glimpse of the private Gus behind closed doors.

There was a pause, and he could see she was trying to make up her mind. Finally she said, "Want to walk up and have a look around?"

Instinctively, Nick knew it wasn't an invitation she issued often or lightly. In fact, he'd bet his next paycheck she'd never invited a man up to her living quarters.

"You're just stalling on the pool, aren't you?"

She laughed. "Absolutely. Busted."

"Me, too." He stood. "I'd love to see your place."

"This way, then." She grabbed her drink and headed toward the door. Opening it, she flipped on the light switch and stepped aside, waving her hand toward the stairs. "After you."

The urge to kiss her again was almost overwhelming but he showed a little self-control and refrained. He didn't want to do a damn thing to spook her when he was so close to being in her private space.

He started up and glanced back over his shoulder, "You just wanted me to go first so you could check out my butt."

Her smile was pure sass. "You wish. Maybe I didn't want you checking out my tush."

"Too late, honey. I'm a guy."

He loved her laugh. She gave him a small push in his back. "Just keep moving."

He moved. "You sure are bossy."

"It comes from being in charge."

He stopped at the door at the top of the stairs.

"It's unlocked," she said. "You can go ahead."

He stepped in and although he shouldn't have been surprised based on what he'd seen and knew about her, he still was.

"Wow." He could've just walked into any loft in the city.

She stepped into the room behind him. "You like it?" She sounded pleased by his astounded reaction.

"It's fantastic. You'd never guess something like this was here in Good Riddance." The place was an open design with the kitchen, dining and living area all together. Where the rest of the room was white, a warm red accented the far wall in the kitchen. Gus had outfitted the kitchen with stainless steel appliances and a pot rack hung over the work island in the center.

A long, large rustic table was lined with chairs. It reminded him of the table at his parents. It was obviously the sign of someone who liked to prepare food for others. Sadly, he wondered if she'd ever entertained anyone up here other than perhaps Merrilee and Bull. He suspected she hadn't. He just hadn't sensed that kind of connection between her and the rest of the twentysomething, thirtysomething crowd in Good Riddance.

He walked over to the table for a closer look, trailing his hand over the surface. "Cool table."

"It was a barn door. Bull was delivering some lumber and they were tearing this down so he salvaged it for me. I love it." She lightly ran her hand over the table and, as if she'd read his mind, said, "I keep saying I'm going to start having Sunday night dinners up here." She shrugged, a hint of melancholy in her smile. "Maybe when the new year comes."

"That's as good a time as any," he said.

He pivoted, checking out the living room. Sleek, contemporary furniture and artwork gave the room a cosmopolitan feel. He liked the mix of modern and rustic.

"There are two bedrooms over there and a bathroom." Gus pointed to an open doorway that opened to a small hall. In one corner a silver tinsel Christmas tree sparkled with tiny white lights.

"Very, very nice," Nick said, walking over to a framed black-and-white photo which had obviously been enlarged. He looked back over his shoulder at Gus, who stood watching him, as if gauging his reaction. "Paris?"

"Yes. I went to school there."

He moved to a collection of framed photographs, two in black-and-white, two in color, of Gus and a woman who was obviously her mother, the resemblance was so striking. They shared the same almond-shaped eyes, striking dark hair, although her mother's was threaded with gray, and that same bow of a mouth. "This has to be your mother."

She moved to stand beside him, looking at the photos. Her smile was wistful and loving. "Yes. I'd just graduated and come back from Paris. We spent a week at the beach together to celebrate before I moved to New York. It was wonderful."

She looked so young and carefree and happy it tore

at his heart because it merely accentuated her wariness now and the shadows that seemed to haunt her eyes.

"I like your house. A lot. You'd never believe you were in the Alaskan wilderness."

She smiled, obviously pleased by his response. "I know. It's my retreat. Have a seat if you'd like."

He settled on the red leather sofa with chrome legs. This was not the home of a woman embracing Alaska. This was the home of a woman trying to replicate an urban lifestyle in the middle of nowhere.

She sat in a chair upholstered in zebra print. She looked very elegant, very sanguine reclining in her black and white chair with her black and white hair, sipping a glass of wine.

"Augustina?"

She regarded him across the top of her wineglass with her almond-shaped eyes. "Why do you call me that?"

"It's your name, isn't it? Does it offend you?"

"No, it doesn't offend me. I'm just curious as to why you'd call me that rather than Gus."

"Because it's sophisticated and complicated and something about it implies layers. It suits you. Gus suits Good Riddance, but I'm not so sure it suits you."

She tilted her head in a mix of consideration and perhaps acknowledgment. "I'd prefer you call me Gus."

"Okay. That's not a problem." He knew, however, that his next question would be a problem. He hoped like hell it wouldn't get him kicked out. But she'd let him in her home so he figured he had a fighting chance.

"Gus, who are you hiding from?"

FREE Merchandise is 'in the Cards' for you!

Dear Reader,

We're giving away FREE MERCHANDISE!

Seriously, we'd like to reward you for reading this novel by giving you **FREE MERCHANDISE** worth over **$20**. And no purchase is necessary!

You see the Jack of Hearts sticker above? Paste that sticker in the box on the Free Merchandise Voucher inside. Return the Voucher promptly...and we'll send you valuable Free Merchandise!

Thanks again for reading one of our novels—and enjoy your Free Merchandise with our compliments!

Pam Powers

Pam Powers

P.S. Look inside to see what Free Merchandise is **"in the cards"** for you!

W
e'd like to send you two free books to introduce you to the Harlequin® Blaze® series. These books are worth over $10, but they are yours to keep absolutely FREE! We'll even send you 2 wonderful surprise gifts. You can't lose!

REMEMBER: Your Free Merchandise, consisting of **2 Free Books** and **2 Free Gifts**, is worth over $20.00! No purchase is necessary, so please send for your Free Merchandise today.

The Reader Service - Here's how it works:

Accepting your 2 free books and 2 free mystery gifts (gifts valued at approximately $10.00) places you under no obligation to buy anything. You may keep the books and gifts and return the shipping statement marked "cancel." If you do not cancel, about a month later we'll send you 6 additional books and bill you just $4.24 each in the U.S. or $4.71 each in Canada. That's a savings of 15% off the cover price. It's quite a bargain! Shipping and handling is just 50¢ per book.* You may cancel at any time, but if you choose to continue, every month we'll send you 6 more books, which you may either purchase at the discount price or return to us and cancel your subscription.

*Terms and prices subject to change without notice. Prices do not include applicable taxes. Sales tax applicable in N.Y. Canadian residents will be charged applicable taxes. Offer not valid in Quebec. All orders subject to approval. Books received may not be as shown. Credit or debit balances in a customer's account(s) may be offset by any other outstanding balance owed by or to the customer. Please allow 4 to 6 weeks for delivery. Offer available while quantities last.

▲ If offer card is missing write to: The Reader Service, P.O. Box 1867, Buffalo, NY 14240-1867 or visit www.ReaderService.com ▲

BUSINESS REPLY MAIL
FIRST-CLASS MAIL   PERMIT NO. 717   BUFFALO, NY

POSTAGE WILL BE PAID BY ADDRESSEE

THE READER SERVICE
PO BOX 1867
BUFFALO NY 14240-9952

NO POSTAGE
NECESSARY
IF MAILED
IN THE
UNITED STATES

8

NICK'S QUESTION DIDN'T surprise her. It was almost a relief to finally have it out on the table rather than constantly hanging in the background. She'd known it was simply a matter of time. He was a smart man and she'd seen the wheels turning since he'd arrived.

"It's been said more than once around here that everyone is either running from something or to something," she finally said.

"You obviously fall into the 'away from' category."

It wasn't a question and it wasn't an indictment; it was simply a statement. Nick sat back on the couch and waited, not expectantly but patiently.

For the longest time after Troy, Gus had questioned her judgment. How could she not have spotted what he was before she got so involved with him? It had taken her four years to begin to believe in her own ability to discern people's character. Nick struck her as a genuinely good guy. And she'd noticed how Clint and Nelson both liked Nick. The two cousins were courteous to almost everyone, but it spoke to a person's character to actually have them embrace someone. They'd embraced Nick. Her gut told her she could trust him, as much as she was willing to trust anyone.

The music playing on the jukebox downstairs drifted up the stairwell. Ah, Lena Horne singing "Stormy Weather," one of Gus's favorites. She slid off her shoes and tucked her feet to one side of the chair.

Nick wanted her story. It no longer made sense not to tell it. She was certain he wouldn't write about her. He'd given his word and he struck her as a man of honor. However, if he wanted to write about her, he would and the truth, while not pretty, was at least preferable to speculation.

The question was, did she have the courage to pull out the monster lurking beneath the bed? She breathed in deeply through her nose, feeling the air fill her lungs, and she slowly exhaled, centering herself. Yes, yes, she did have the courage.

Where to begin?

She sipped at her wine and finally looked up. Nick sat patiently, waiting. She started with the easy stuff, the good stuff. "I knew from the time I was a kid and was running three Easy-Bake Ovens at a time and all the neighborhood kids were sitting around waiting for what I was making that I wanted to be a chef." She pointed to the print of Paris on the opposite wall. "I trained in Paris, which I loved, and then I went to New York. I did fairly well there." He was from New York. Nick would know that fairly well meant her career had gotten off to a stellar start.

She drew a deep breath. Now the monster would

come out in the open. "One day a customer wanted to meet me because he'd been particularly impressed by a dish I'd prepared."

"Do you remember the dish?" Nick asked.

She smiled at the question, relieved by the mundaneness of it. "You would think I would, but I don't. We were terribly busy that day—" she laughed when she remembered the hectic, rushed kitchen "—we were busy every day, but when a customer's impressed you take the time to chat, so I chatted."

"And he was more struck by you than the dish and asked you out," Nick said.

"Predictable, isn't it, but yes." She tucked her hair behind her ear.

"He became your fiancé?"

She glanced sharply at him and he shrugged. "Pure speculation on my part."

Her heart began to hammer against her ribs. Spooked, she pressed him. "But how did you know that? All I said was that I had been engaged and it didn't work out."

"It was the way you said it. You were completely blank. People are only that way when they have something to hide. That was my clue."

She'd remember that moving forward. Feeling calmer, she nodded and continued. "Yes. Eight months later we were engaged." She traced the edge of her glass with her fingertip. "Maybe it was the new wearing off or maybe it was just that men like him can only keep the facade up for so long and then their true colors start to come through."

"Controlling? Demanding?"

She nodded. Unfortunately, hers really wasn't a unique story. "It was just little things at first and then it seemed to escalate. My relationship with him was beginning to impact my work. I wasn't happy so I broke off the engagement…and yes, I returned the ring." He'd refused to take it back so she'd finally couriered it to him at his office.

"But it wasn't over, was it?" Nick leaned forward, bracing his forearms on his knees. "Because he was in control and it was up to him to decide if and when it would end."

Nick understood, he got it. Relieved, she nodded. "He harassed me. He'd wait for me after work. He broke into my apartment, or had it broken into, several times. He'd leave flowers along with threatening notes." That had been the worst—the juxtaposition of beauty with malice. She didn't think she'd ever feel the same about fresh-cut flowers again. "At first I was outraged but then it escalated and became frightening. The worst was when I came in and he'd slashed my sheets and mattress with a knife and poured red paint all over it to look like blood." There, she'd finally said it, given it voice. She shuddered but it was something of a relief to tell someone else.

Nick clenched his fists and his face grew tight. "Son of a bitch."

"I never slept in that bed again. I'd sleep on the couch." She could barely stand to go into her apartment anymore at that point, always uncertain of what or who she'd find there.

"You don't have to answer this if you don't want to,

but did he ever physically assault you?" Nick asked, training his eyes on the rug, giving her privacy even though he sat across from her.

Old feelings of degradation and humiliation surfaced. She'd never been hit before. She'd been so surprised the first time. "Yes." She simply couldn't bear to say any more about that aspect of it.

This time he was the one who drew a deep breath before speaking. "The police?"

"I went several times." That had been its own little mini-nightmare. "His family is powerful and well connected. My third time there, they were treating me as if I was the one at fault for wasting their time and slandering this man. And the more he got away with, the more it escalated. I finally quit my job, gave up my apartment, and moved out of state. I thought if I put some distance between us, out of sight out of mind, that he'd let it go, let me go."

She could see Nick struggle to maintain a neutral expression, but the more she talked, the tighter his face became. "Where'd you move? What'd you do?"

"I bought a car and through connections in the restaurant business, I got a job in Northern Virginia, an affluent area with some very high-end restaurants. I moved into a gated community and thought it was over. I was starting over and I finally felt safe again. It's interesting how much we take safety for granted until it's compromised."

"He found you." There was a grimness about Nick when he spoke that showed another side of him. He was charming and easy to be around but given the right circumstances, Nick would also be a force to be reckoned with. "Credit card? Car registration?"

"Likely both. He definitely found me." A faint shudder ran through her. "It was my day off and I'd been down to the farmer's market and picked up fresh fish and vegetables for dinner. And a bouquet of sunflowers because they're happy—isn't it funny the details that stick with you. I was in the kitchen when he simply walked in. He was wearing a blue shirt and a terrifying smile. I remember thinking blue was supposed to represent tranquillity."

"There is no out of sight out of mind with men like him."

"No. I realized that. The way I saw it, I had two choices, I could go back to him or continue to let him stalk me and one of us was going to die, probably me, or I could try to outsmart and outrun him. I ran."

NICK THOUGHT HE COULD single-handedly rip the bastard apart when he found him. And make no mistake, he would find him. "And you eventually wound up here."

"Eventually. I packed two large suitcases, two garbage bags, threw them in my car and left. The woman I was the night I left Northern Virginia no longer exists. Literally. Which is why you couldn't find me when you googled me."

"You knew I did that?"

"Of course you would." Her hint of a smile told him it was okay. "I knew you were curious. You work for a news organization."

He'd been right, but he hadn't known just how dangerous the man she was running from was. She had been up against formidable odds if his family had enough influence and power to control the cops.

He recalled his initial conversation with Teddy and Merrilee when Teddy had told him her boss was a chef from New York, and he'd said it would make an interesting story. "You've spent the last four years looking over your shoulder and then I show up blogging for the *Times*." He paused and looked into her gray eyes, wanting to reassure her. "I'm not going to compromise your safety, Gus. I would never, ever do anything to put you in danger."

She regarded him solemnly. "Do you think I would have told you all of this if I thought you would? I'm very cautious."

He felt as if he'd been given a gift. This amazing woman who had run for her life had decided to trust him, confide in him. "I know that. It means a lot to me." He paused and then asked another question, one he simply couldn't help but ask. "Who were you before?"

"It simply doesn't matter, Nick." She shook her head. "That woman is dead and buried."

"No, she's not. She's been locked away but I don't believe for a moment she's dead and buried." No doubt about it, Nick would like some time alone with this guy in a dark alley. "Who is this bastard?"

"I'm not giving you his name." The look in her eyes said there was no compromise, no backing down on that point. "The police couldn't do anything. You start nosing around and I'm sunk. You ask questions and he'll know.

He reads your columns and it would be easy enough to figure out from there. Even if it weren't easy, he'd figure it out, he's smart."

Nick was no longer simply curious, he was desperate to know, to help her. "Then give me his name. I have friends that can be trusted. They can look. You know just because you're not available doesn't mean he's changed or stopped. Other women are going through what he put you through, or worse. He has to be stopped, Gus." Otherwise he would forever hold this woman prisoner in this cell of her own making. She'd escaped him, but he continued to control her.

She rubbed at her forehead, as if she was weary beyond words, then she lifted her chin. "I've thought about that, but you don't understand—" she paused for emphasis "—the police did *nothing*."

She'd been thwarted at every turn. He ran his hands through his hair in frustration. The pictures on the wall distracted him and yet another piece of the puzzle fell into place. There wasn't the faintest resemblance between Gus's mother and the woman who was supposed to be her aunt. And whoever this piece of shit was, he would've known about her family members and the game would've been up long ago.

"Merrilee isn't really your aunt, is she? Otherwise he would've found you by now."

"No." She offered a faint smile acknowledging he'd figured it out. "She's not my aunt, but she's like family. She and my mother grew up together in Georgia. She's all the family I have now."

"Your parents?"

"My father and mother divorced when I was young. He remarried and he was good about sending a check, but that was it. Diane, the new wife, didn't want me around and that was the way it was." She shrugged but he didn't believe for a moment her father's lack of involvement didn't hurt. "My mother died the year I graduated from culinary school. I was glad she saw me graduate."

She looked over at the photos on the wall. "I was fortunate we had that time together. It was before we knew she was sick and then she went fast, which she always maintained was a blessing. She said her one regret was that I'd be left alone—it had only been the two of us for so long." Her voice thickened and her eyes watered. She paused, visibly pulling herself together and he was amazed by her fortitude. Did she have any idea what a strong person she was? He wanted nothing more at that moment than to gather her up and drop her into the middle of his big, boisterous family so they could love her.

Gus bit her bottom lip and then, once again in control, continued. "Merrilee came to the funeral. It was the first time I'd seen her since I was twelve or thirteen."

Nick was trying to piece it all together in his head and she didn't seem to mind answering questions. Actually, the questions she didn't want to answer, she simply didn't. "How long was it after you lost your mother that you met this man?"

"A year and two weeks. I'd thrown myself into my work. She and I weren't just mother and daughter. We were friends and confidantes and I missed her like crazy. I still miss her."

"I can't imagine." And he couldn't. His parents had always been there for him. They gave him roots.

"Tr—he didn't know about Merrilee. I'd seen her at the funeral and she'd told me to keep in touch but it was just too painful and I didn't. It's funny, the night I packed my stuff and left Northern Virginia, I didn't have a plan. I drove as far as I could and slept in a Wal-Mart parking lot with the motor home group."

He didn't know what she was talking about. He obviously looked perplexed, because she explained.

"Wal-Mart allows motor homes to overnight in their parking lots. They can pull in there and spend the night in their campers if they want to. I just parked behind one so at first glance it'd look as if I was a car being towed behind it. Anyway, when I woke up the next morning, I thought of Merrilee. She just popped into my head. I went into the store, bought a prepaid cell phone and tracked her down that way. I stayed in a cheap motel and Bull came and got me."

It was damn near impossible to imagine the woman sitting across from him sleeping in a parking lot with all her worldly possessions loaded into a car, having to contact virtual strangers for help. "Had you ever met Bull before?"

"Once, at my mother's funeral, but I can't say that any of that was very clear."

"So, Bull came for you and you vanished without a trace? That's not easy to do these days."

"It's not easy, but it's possible." She smiled and again

he was overwhelmed by her courage. "Unless you get your picture and your name mentioned in the *Times*."

"Augustina's your real name but not Tippens, am I right?"

"Yes. I was named after my mother's favorite aunt. But my full name only ever came into play on official documents."

"And you're not going to tell me your real name, are you?" It was rhetorical. He knew that answer as surely as he knew his own name.

"No, because it doesn't matter. This is who I am now, this is where I belong. I don't know what I would have done without Merrilee, Bull and Good Riddance. This is my haven."

Nick would beg to differ. It was as clear as the nose on his face. She didn't belong here, but that was a realization she'd have to come to herself. "Thank you for telling me your story. It's safe with me."

"I thought it would be, otherwise you would've never heard it." She sipped at her wine.

"It's late and I know that wasn't easy for you. Do you want me to go?" God knows he didn't want to leave, he'd never wanted to stay more, but he didn't want to crowd her or rush her. And he sure as hell didn't want to take advantage of her when she was emotionally vulnerable so he was giving her an out if she wanted to take it.

For a second she looked totally unsure of herself and horribly vulnerable. "Do you want to leave? Did what I told you change things for you?"

She thought her story had turned him off? That *he* was looking for an out? They'd get this straight pronto.

"No. I don't want to leave. I've never wanted to stay with a woman more, but I don't want you to have any regrets or feel as if I took advantage of you." She started to say something, but he held up his hand to cut her off. He needed to finish what he wanted to say. "Yes, your story did change things for me." Confusion flitted across her face. "I liked you, respected you before, but that's all deeper and stronger now. We're all the sum of our experiences and you are one hell of a woman and I think I'm damn lucky to be sitting here with you now."

"I think…that's the sweetest thing anyone's ever said to me."

"It's the truth."

"I appreciate your sensitivity, Nick, but it's the past. I cleared the air and I don't want to think about him anymore, especially right now." The look in her eyes told Nick exactly what she wanted.

Him.

9

IT WAS AMAZING HOW MUCH BETTER she felt getting that out of the way. Troy was still a monster and he remained a threat, but there was something empowering about dragging him out in the open.

"I'm going to follow your lead," Nick said. "You set the pace. This is your call. We'll go as far and as fast as you want to. When we've hit *your* limit, we've hit *my* limit."

Even though it felt awkward to get out of her chair and move to sit next to Nick on the couch, Gus appreciated his sensitivity. Placing her wineglass on the coffee table, she canted toward him on the sofa. She'd known the searing heat, the slow simmer, and now they were on medium, which felt just right. She didn't want to rush this with him.

He reached over and cupped her jaw in his hand, tracing the ridge of her cheekbone with his thumb. "I wanted you from the first moment I caught a glimpse of you."

He lowered his head and pressed a kiss to her neck,

sending a spear of heat through her. "I felt bad for Teddy when she got sick—" another nuzzle against her throat "—but I was glad it gave me a chance to spend time with you because otherwise I was sunk."

He nibbled at her neck sending the most delicious sensations coursing along her nerve endings.

"You're shameless," she said, her breath catching in her throat when he teased his tongue against the lower lobe of her ear.

He nipped. "I know."

It had been so long since she'd been with a man, having Nick's mouth and breath play against her skin was like standing in a sweet downpour after four years of drought. She reveled in the erotic scrape of his whiskers against her neck, her face. And it wasn't just any man, it was important to her that it was this man. A man who knew when to laugh but also knew how to listen, and was strong enough to step back and give her the space she needed to make this special.

She buried her fingers in his hair, luxuriating in the sensation against her skin. He trailed his lips across her jaw until his mouth claimed hers. His slow, languid kiss sipped, explored, delved, over and over until she felt as if she was floating, buoyed by their kisses.

She sensed his restraint, felt it in the taut line of his body. He was truly leaving it up to her to set the pace. He was one of a kind and she was indescribably glad she'd waited for *him* to land on her doorstep. There was no one she'd rather be here with now than Nick.

"Relax," she said. "I promise I won't break."

"Good," he murmured against her jaw. "I don't want

you to break. I just want you to fall apart…when the time comes."

She leaned into him, pushing him back onto the couch, landing on top of him. Gus deepened their kiss, intensified it, her tongue seeking his.

He made a satisfied sound against her mouth that only notched up her pleasure in the feel of him beneath her, his tongue dancing intimately with hers. Nick rubbed his hands up and down her back, kneading, stroking. His touch felt so good. The aching want between her thighs intensified to need.

She wanted the slide of his hands over her skin, the press of his bare flesh against hers. Without breaking her mouth from his, she sat up enough to tug his shirt loose and run her hands beneath the fabric. She plied her hands against solid male flesh and moaned into his mouth. Touching him brought a pleasure all its own.

He worked his hands beneath the hem of her top and stroked her back with his strong, sure hands.

They were still fully clothed and she was absolutely burning for him. Based on the ridge of his arousal cradled between her thighs, he was equally hot for her.

She sat up, her breathing uneven. "Nick, let's go to my bedroom."

"If you're sure that's what you want." He brushed the backs of his fingers against her belly and she sucked in a sharp breath at the sensation quivering through her. "I don't need to be asked twice."

She slid off of him and stood by the couch. Holding her hand out, she said, "I've never been surer." And she hadn't.

Hand in hand they went into her bedroom. He wrapped his arms around her from behind, pulling her close to rest against his solidness. She relaxed into him, absorbing the feel of his chest against her shoulders, his abs against her back, his arousal against her buttocks.

She turned her head and pressed a kiss to his bicep then nuzzled her cheek against the hard muscle. His scent, surrounding her as surely as his arms, was intoxicating—unique.

He stroked his hands over her shirt-covered middle and nipped at the sensitive back of her neck, his mouth sending the heat inside her spiraling out of control. She sighed and leaned her head against his shoulder, granting him closer access to her neck and shoulder. His breath whispered across her skin, followed by his lips and the tender stroking of his tongue. Sweet, wet heat flooded her.

Nick turned her around to face him. Gus stepped back to the bed and, taking his hands, pulled him down beside her. The room lay in shadows except for the light spilling in from the den. That worked for her. It had been a long, long time since she'd been naked in front of anyone.

He rolled into her, cupping her head in his hand and kissing her again. His mouth felt like magic against hers. Gus slid her fingers beneath his shirt, over the expanse of his back. She loved the way his skin felt beneath her hand. Slowly, taking their time, they undressed one another until they were lying in her darkened bedroom in their underwear. She looked her fill.

Nick was, in a word, beautiful. If she had conjured

up a recipe for the perfect male specimen, he was exactly what she would have gotten. Broad shoulders, well-defined biceps—somewhere he found time to visit a gym because he didn't come by those typing on a computer or boarding an airplane—narrow hips, and muscular legs.

However, it was his chest and belly that totally did her in. For whatever reason known only to God and advertising executives, sexy men were now portrayed with totally hairless bodies. That just didn't work for her. Men were supposed to look like men. And Nick looked like a man. Dark, curling hair covered his chest and ran down his belly to his sex. He wasn't gorilla man, which would have turned her off. He was simply her man, which turned her on.

He skimmed his hand down her side, over her hip and she sucked in an unsteady breath.

"Your skin is so soft," Nick said. "You feel so good."

"I like it when you touch me."

"Can I take your bra off?"

"Yes. I want to feel your hands on me—your mouth on me."

"Honey, that is not a problem. If that's what you want, that's what you'll get."

His words and his touch enflamed her. The cooler air settled against her skin when he slipped her bra off. He paused for a moment. "Wow."

Gus smiled. "Is that a good wow?"

"You damn well better believe it is." He gathered

her breasts in his hands, brushing his thumbs over her nipples.

"Oh, wow," she gasped.

He followed his hands with his mouth. Gus arched off of the mattress when he tugged her nipple into his warm, wet mouth and sucked. He gave the same attention to the other one and she was awash in the need to feel him between her thighs. She'd wanted to go slow but urgency gripped her. She reached between them and stroked his erection that was straining against the front of his briefs.

"Gus." Her name came out as a gasp.

"Yes. Now."

He rustled around in his jeans pocket until he pulled out a condom. While he divested himself of his underwear, Gus slipped her panties off. She didn't need any additional foreplay. She was more than ready for him.

He rolled to his back, bringing her on top of him. With his hands grasping her hips, Gus straddled him and eased down, taking him inside her, inch by inch. She threw her head back, reveling in the feel of him inside her, filling her. She stilled, savoring the moment.

"You," she said, "on top."

Within seconds, he'd flipped her to her back, reversing positions. "Better?"

"Yes." Oh. Yes. He felt so good inside her.

Nick pistoned up and down, leaning forward to bring his penis into mind-boggling contact with her clit. His mouth found hers and devoured her in an equally mind-numbing kiss.

She felt herself coming undone, piece by piece,

stroke by stroke, until spasms wracked her and she shattered as she called his name.

NICK RETURNED TO THE DARKENED bedroom. While he'd been in the bathroom cleaning up, Gus had pulled back the cover and was between the sheets. Now that the heat of the moment had passed, the room held a chill.

She lifted the edge of the sheet and blanket. "Climb in."

"Don't mind if I do." He slid into bed with her and propped up on one arm. Gus lay on her back, a satisfied smile on her face. It was damn nice to know he was the one who'd put it there. He smoothed her hair back from her face then skimmed his fingers across the satin skin of her cheekbone. "Are you okay?"

"I'm better than okay. I'm great. How about you?"

He put his arm around her and pulled her close to his side. "I'm better than great and damn glad to be here."

He was fairly certain he was the first since the disaster with her fiancé. He was damn certain he was the first man to be here with her in this apartment in this bed—and he liked that. A lot.

"I'm pretty glad you're here," she said, sliding her leg over his and tracing his calf with her instep. She settled her head on his bare chest. He liked the way she felt against him, as if it was where she belonged.

"Gus?"

"Yes?"

He stroked his hand down her back, learning the sweet curve, trailing his fingers along the indent of her spine. "Just a name." He wouldn't rest, know a moment's peace until he tracked the bastard down. "Just give me a name."

"No." She flicked her tongue against his right nipple and the feeling shot straight through to his dick.

He struggled for focus. "But—"

"I don't want him here in the bed with us now." She swirled her tongue over his nipple again, seriously catching his attention. "This is between you and me. And you're only going to be here a few days so we have lots of ground to cover." She trailed her hand down his belly and teased the base of his shaft. "Can we please leave him out of this?"

"Absolutely." For now.

Wrapping her hand around him, she stroked. "Good answer."

"Where do you want me this time?" He still wanted to make sure she was comfortable with where they were, what they did.

"On top, beside, behind…all of it works for me."

Her openness and enthusiasm was a turn-on. Hell, everything about her was a turn-on. He'd never met a woman quite like her before. She was a mix of pragmatic reality and sensual eroticism. It was an intriguing, heady combination.

Nick was ready. He could simply climb on top, behind or beside, as she'd so arousingly put it, and they'd both have a good time but he wanted more than that. He wanted to learn her nuances. He wanted to carry every curve and sigh with him when he left. And he wanted to be the lover she remembered long after he was gone.

"Duly noted and all in good time. You have the

sexiest mouth." He traced the bow of her upper lip with his finger tip. "This drives me crazy."

She smiled against his finger. "Crazy? Really?"

He grinned down at her. "Bonafide madness. It's terrible." He cupped her jaw in his hand and leaned down to kiss her. Her mouth felt and tasted as if it had been custom-made for him. Gus wrapped her arms around his neck and pulled him closer to her. He loved the feel of her satin skin against his.

Moving from her lips, he traced a line of kisses down her neck, her shoulder, down her arm to the delicate inside of her elbow and farther to her wrist.

She sighed beneath him. He traveled to the tender skin of her belly and past to the rounded curve of her hip where he discovered the sensitive spot between her hip and pubic area. He pressed kisses against the inside of her thigh, inhaling the scent of her sex.

"Oh, yes," she murmured.

That was all the encouragement he needed. He spread her thighs further apart, opening her to him. He teased his tongue along the folds of her sex and she canted her hips up off of the bed, issuing a moan. He would be inside her again later but now, this was exactly what he wanted and where he wanted to be, lapping at her, tasting her. And apparently it was precisely where she wanted him, as well.

"CAN I STAY THE NIGHT?" Nick asked, his profile etched in the light from the other room as he lay back against her pillow. He looked frighteningly right there.

"Not tonight," she said. She needed time to think, to

regroup. She thought perhaps she wanted him to stay another time but not now. "Maybe tomorrow night. Let's talk about it then." That afforded her time to marshal her thoughts. "Plus, I'm worn out—" she grinned at him "—in a good way, but tired still. I'm not used to sleeping with anyone and I need some sleep tonight."

"It's okay. I know when I'm being kicked to the curb." His grin told her he was teasing.

Not only was the man great in bed, he had a sense of humor. That was a double bonus in her book. Actually, make it a triple because he knew his way around a kitchen as effectively as he knew his way around a bedroom.

"Consider yourself kicked."

"Ouch."

She laughed. She liked this silly give and take with him. Maybe he was so easy to be with because there was no future relationship at stake. Another part of her whispered that maybe he was so easy to be with because he was the right man for her.

"Go ahead and laugh, you cold woman."

She trailed her fingers over his chest. "You weren't complaining about me being cold half an hour ago."

"Honey, you were anything but cold. I thought we might burn the place down." He slid out of bed and pulled on his underwear. Gus watched. This just didn't happen often in her world—by her choice, but it still didn't happen, nonetheless. She was looking while she could look. Still watching him, she threw off the covers and started pulling on her clothes as well, skipping her bra.

"You don't have to get dressed," he said. "I can see myself out."

"I don't mind seeing you out and I need to shut down everything downstairs anyway."

Gus couldn't remember ever feeling this comfortable with anyone. There was none of that awkwardness she'd experienced in the past immediately after sex. Even when she and Troy had been engaged, sometimes after they'd been in bed together it had been uncomfortable at times.

She tugged her shirt over her head at the same time he finished buckling his belt.

"Ready?" he said.

"Ready."

He slipped on his shoes, carrying his socks in his hands. They were quiet going downstairs and neither spoke until they reached the door connecting her place to Merrilee's. He wrapped his arms around her and held her close. "Thank you for tonight."

She buried her face in his neck, inhaling his scent, knowing it would be on her sheets when she returned to bed. "I enjoyed it, too."

"Meet me for breakfast in the morning."

She was flattered he wanted to spend time with her again so soon. "I could do that."

"Okay, I'm just going to be bold and ask if there's any chance we could have breakfast in your apartment. Privacy is in short order here."

He'd nailed the privacy issue. "That works for me. Sometimes living here is like living under a microscope. In fact, tomorrow morning, if you go outside, you'll see a set of stairs on the back corner of the building. That leads to my apartment. Merrilee has the same thing on her side. It's a safety issue in case of fire. Come over around eight and I'll have the door unlocked. Just come on in."

"I'm already looking forward to it." He traced his thumb over her cheekbone and she quivered deep inside at the sweetness, the tenderness behind that gesture. And then because food was what she did, she asked, "What would you like for breakfast?"

His grin held more than a hint of devilment. "Honey, I don't care whether we eat or not."

"But if we're not eating what will we do?" Her tone was pure innocence.

"I think we'll find something to occupy the time."

10

GUS BEAT HER ALARM CLOCK the following morning. She was up and out of bed before it even had a chance to ring. She felt like a teenager again. Actually, she wasn't sure whether she'd ever felt this giddy, even when she was a teenager. She'd gone to sleep thinking of Nick and woken up thinking of him. With a start she realized for the first time in over four years, Troy hadn't crept into her thoughts last night. Maybe it was because she'd realized last night she was tired of running. She'd been running for the last four years, even though she'd been right here. If Nick had figured out everything else, he would sooner than later figure out Troy's identity. But there'd be no more running on her part. Let the chips fall where they may. For the first time in over four years, she finally, finally, felt in control of her own life again. It was liberating, exhilarating.

She gave her mind free reign while she prepped breakfast. Nick might not want to eat when he got here—in fact, she couldn't wait to get her hands on him again and she was planning on going straight to the bedroom—but they would eat eventually.

He'd been so sweet when he'd asked to stay the night and she wasn't being coy when she'd sent him away—she just hadn't been mentally prepared to have him stay. Nothing was secret in Good Riddance. But then again, people were incredibly curious here, but also very accepting. It wasn't as if she stood to scandalize the entire town. It had taken four years for a man like Nick Hudson to cross her path. God knows how long it would take for another one to show up on her doorstep.

Ever since she'd arrived she'd poured herself into the restaurant. Sophisticated, funny, roll-up-his-shirtsleeves-and-jump-in-to-help Nick was like a flash of springtime in the dead of winter. She felt more alive and energized than she had in longer than she could remember. So, Gus Tippens was going to rock the boat. Gus was going to go for broke and tell Nick he could do more than just stay one night, he could stay with her until he left. She was going to temporarily claim her own man here in Good Riddance.

And speaking of claiming as her own, she realized she'd forgotten all about Jenna's request once again. She checked her watch. Nick shouldn't be here for another forty minutes or so.

Gus paced back and forth in her apartment kitchen—she'd always done her best thinking in front of a stove or countertop. Jenna wanted a recipe to attract a particular animal so she'd be marked in the native tradition and she'd then be acceptable to Nelson and his tribe. And like a dummy Gus had blithely agreed without thinking it through.

She couldn't give Jenna a recipe. It was dangerous and wrong to try to feed or attract wild animals. Everyone in this part of the country knew that—well, Chris of Chrismoose fame had been the exception but Alaska was all about exceptions.

Actually coming up with a recipe for Jenna would've been the easier thing to do. Instead, what Gus had to do now was face Jenna and bring her down as gently as possible.

And then Jenna needed to have a conversation with Nelson. She felt bad for Jenna—this situation had broken heart written all over it—but Gus didn't see any other way around it. She was not looking forward to taking this up with Jenna, especially with the Chrismoose pageant scheduled for tonight.

A brief knock sounded on the outer door, which she'd unlocked earlier, and then Nick opened it and stepped inside. Outside, snow swirled in the dark morning. He closed the door. Snowflakes clung to his dark hair and dusted the shoulders of his jacket.

Something indefinable surged through her at the sight of him. "Hi."

"Hi."

His smile sent another surge through her and she realized it was happiness—pure, unadulterated joy at seeing him. "Any trouble finding the place?" she asked, teasing.

He grinned as he shrugged out of his coat and hung it on the peg next to the door. "I only got lost twice."

She started toward him. "I'm glad you made it."

"Me, too." He bridged the rest of the distance.

And then that was all she wrote. They were on one another as if they couldn't stay away...and Gus was sure she couldn't. Last night had been about taking their time. This morning that wasn't an issue. Kissing frantically, they somehow managed to stumble their way to the bedroom. Nick fell back on the mattress, pulling her down on top of him.

Yes, breakfast would definitely be delayed for a while.

NICK SAT ACROSS THE TABLE from Gus and had the frightening thought that he could definitely get used to sitting across from her in the mornings. Her hair was a bit of a mess but he liked it for two reasons. One, he was responsible for it being in that state and two, he liked the fact that she didn't fuss over her appearance. They'd climbed out of bed and she'd run her fingers through it and headed for the kitchen.

"Great breakfast," he said, savoring the last bite.

"I'm glad you liked it."

She'd made an egg dish with spinach, artichoke hearts, and a sauce served with fruit and a sourdough Asiago cheese toast. "You really have a talent."

"Thank you. You know I think you do, as well."

She'd told him once before she liked his blog and that meant a lot to him. The inhabitants of Good Riddance were extremely fortunate to have her restaurant but... "Do you really see yourself staying here indefinitely?"

She shrugged and began to clear the dishes. He started to rise to help and she waved him back down. "I've made my spot here."

She stacked the dishes in the sink and returned to the table.

"How do I say this delicately?" Nick steepled his fingers. He was seldom at a loss to express himself. Hell, there was nothing for it but to throw it out there. "I like this town but you're too big for it. Your talent's too big for it."

A frown played between her eyebrows and he truly hoped he hadn't overstepped his bounds but it felt as if they'd cut through so much of the bullshit people waded through and danced around. However, there was still a good chance she'd tell him it was none of his damn business.

She picked up her coffee cup but didn't drink from it. "I don't know quite how to explain it, but when I first got here I was sort of in survival mode. And then I threw myself into remodeling the restaurant and making it as successful as I could. I've been so busy with the here and now, I haven't given the long-term future much thought."

"If you could leave tomorrow, would you? If it was just for a short trip, a vacation?" He sensed a longing and a restlessness in her he wasn't sure she was even aware of. Which might have sounded presumptuous but he felt this weird connection with this woman he'd never experienced with anyone else.

"I took a couple of days off and spent some time in Anchorage last year."

He glanced pointedly at the framed pictures of Paris and New York on her walls. "I meant outside the state of Alaska."

Her smile held an edge. "Yes, it would be nice to travel. But I've explained my situation to you."

He nodded. He couldn't imagine always looking over his shoulder for a stalker. But he also couldn't imagine spending the rest of his life in hiding. It didn't seem any way to live to him.

"What about you?" she said. "Don't you ever get tired of roaming the world? Don't you ever think of settling down?"

"Every now and then, but I'm not ready. There are still lots of places to go and see." He had thought on occasion, and it seemed more frequently lately, that sometimes it would be nice to have a travel companion, but then again that could easily turn into an anchor. "I sort of have the best of both worlds. My family is always there when I'm in New York and in the meantime, I get to see the world."

She stood without commenting and crossed to the sink where she poured the rest of her coffee down the drain, then rinsed the cup.

And he was suddenly very much aware he had another three days with this woman and then he was heading home for Christmas and she was staying here. He rose from the table and slid his arms around her from behind. "Breakfast was great." He kissed the back of her neck. "I'm glad I invited myself."

She laughed and turned to face him. Leaning back against the sink, she linked her arms around his waist.

"Speaking of invites, I have one for you." She lowered her gaze and seemed to have developed a sudden fascination with his shirt. "I've thought about it and you can stay here the rest of your trip if you want to."

"If I want to?" He felt as if he'd just been handed an early Christmas present. He couldn't contain his grin. "Hmm, let me think about it." He pretended to ponder. "Let's see, sleeping alone next door and sharing a bathroom with six other people or sleeping with you and sharing a bathroom with you? I think I want to."

She narrowed her eyes at him in mock outrage. "I see how it goes. You only want me for my bathroom facilities."

Nick grew serious. He knew her well enough to know she hadn't issued that invitation lightly. He was honored. Smoothing his thumb over her cheek bone, he said, "Honey, I'd stay with you even if you didn't have a bathroom."

Her eyes smiled into his and it was like standing in the warm sun. "Luckily, I do." She released him. "I'm going to take care of the dishes."

"I'll help," he said.

She sent him another one of her radiant smiles. "Okay. I'll wash. You dry."

They worked well together. He'd noticed it the two days he'd worked in the restaurant with her. She began filling the sink.

"You're okay with people talking?" he asked.

Gus laughed as the suds began to form. "People are going to talk regardless. So I'll be the one giving them something to talk about this time around." She grinned.

"After four years, it's my turn to pull the gossip train. It's probably all over town already that you're here now. I'm sure someone, somewhere saw you coming up those outer stairs."

"Merrilee's not going to be happy. She doesn't like me."

"No, she doesn't like you." She tossed him a dish towel and then plunged her hands into the soapy water. "You scare her. All you have to do is post something about me or the restaurant and I'm done."

"I've told you that's not going to happen. You can trust me."

"If I didn't trust you, you wouldn't be here now."

"What does she think I'd have to gain by exposing you?"

She hesitated for a moment. "His family is well-known."

Nick rinsed what she washed and stacked the dishes on the counter. "Ah, so one of those celebrity exposés in which the out-of-control son sends a woman into hiding."

"Something like that."

"Not going to happen, Gus." He made quick work of drying.

"I know that, Nick. You asked and I'm just telling you where Merrilee is coming from. And no, she won't be happy with me, but I'm an adult."

"I don't want to complicate your life."

"Too late—" she grinned "—but my life needed a little complication." She finished up the last of the pans.

"I'll pack my stuff this morning after I get back from

the snowmobile races." He wanted to spend as much time with her as possible.

"That's fine and I'll handle Merrilee."

Nick winced. "I'm definitely getting the better end of that deal."

LATER THAT MORNING, Merrilee beat Gus to the punch by showing up at her apartment.

"Come on in," Gus said, stepping aside. The breakfast dishes had been put away, but the placemats were still on the table. Obviously two people had eaten at her table. Merrilee's sharp gaze took it all in. "Can I get you a cup of coffee?"

"Thanks but no thanks. We need to talk, Gus."

This was not going to be a good conversation. "Okay," Gus said, walking into the den. She sat in the zebra chair, leaving Merrilee the couch.

Merrilee perched stiffly on the sofa's edge. "You know I'm not one to beat around the bush."

Gus merely nodded and Merrilee continued, "You know I love you and I'm here because I know what time Nick came in this morning and I assume he's the one who ate breakfast with you."

She'd known Merrilee would know, but Gus had to say she felt a bit defensive at having Merrilee tracking her movements. "He is."

"I'm worried." And Gus knew it was true. Merrilee looked tired and there were circles under her eyes. "You're making a big mistake, Gus. You've worked so hard to get yourself to this point but with him you're so vulnerable. He's a reporter."

"Merrilee, I hear what you're saying but I believe I can trust him."

Merrilee rubbed her fingers across her forehead as if to ward off a headache. "Honey...Gus...listen to yourself. Your telling me you can trust a man you've known for a whopping two days? After all you've been through? That alone tells me you're not thinking clearly."

There was no way around it—Merrilee had just hurt her feelings up one side and down the other. She'd never felt the older woman's censure before and it wasn't a good feeling. Gus lifted her chin. "I disagree with you. It's true, I only met him two days ago but I knew him long before that, Merrilee. I read his blogs for nearly two years. You get to know the measure of a man through his work and after meeting him and spending time with him, he is who he comes across as in those columns. I know you have a bad opinion of reporters. I had a bad experience with the police when they wouldn't do anything about Troy, but it doesn't mean all cops aren't trustworthy."

"Gus, I've supported you unfailingly in the past but I can't support you getting close to Nick. You, me, Bull, we all decided the best plan was for you to fly as low as possible under his radar." Merrilee leaned forward in supplication. "I'm begging you to come to your senses and cut it off now before you have a disaster on your hands and everything blows up in our faces."

Gus didn't know how to get Merrilee to see Nick as Gus saw him, knew him. "I just don't think that's going to happen." While they were having this terse discussion, Gus decided she might as well break the rest of the news to Merrilee. She deserved to know. "He knows about Troy. He knows the story. He'd already figured most of it out."

"Oh, dear God." Merrilee literally blanched.

"No, no, no. I'm sorry to have scared you so. He doesn't know Troy's name and he doesn't know my real name. He just knows the story, which, unfortunately, isn't all that different from too many other women's stories."

Merrilee held her hands up, shaking them. "That's what I'm telling you. He's a reporter. He figured that much out. How long do you think it'll take him to figure out Troy's identity? Does he know the police didn't do a damn thing?"

"Yes."

"Families with that kind of influence and power aren't a dime a dozen, Gus. It may not be today or tomorrow but he'll figure it out because he won't be able to leave it alone. It'll gnaw at him until he does."

"That's true. I agree, he's curious about everything. And he's smart, so eventually he will figure it out."

"And you really think he'll just let it go? One of New York's most prominent political families has a son who's a psychopathic stalker and a *Times* reporter will just walk away from *that* story? You're giving him way too much control over your life. Aren't you the one who swore she'd never give control to anyone else?"

"Merrilee, I didn't send the man a personal invitation to come and blog about Chrismoose. He showed up. That was outside of my control. I didn't invite him into my kitchen. I didn't give him any information he hadn't

already figured out. That was outside of my control. At
this point, what difference does keeping him at arm's
length make? It's not going to stop what's already in
motion. It's not going to change a thing."

"If the devil comes dancing on your doorstep, you
don't have to climb in bed with him. I can't support you
in this."

Gus weighed Merrilee's words and her reaction carefully. She would not be emotionally blackmailed into
making a decision just because Merrilee thought it was
the thing to do. Offering her opinion was one thing
but making her support conditional crossed the line for
Gus.

"I hate it that you feel that way, Merrilee."

"So, you're still going to continue to see Nick until
he leaves?"

"I am." She took a deep breath. "He's going to stay
with me for the rest of the time he's here."

Merrilee nodded, her lips held tight in disapproval.
"Well, I guess there's nothing more to be said then."

"I appreciate your concern."

"But apparently not enough to heed my warning."
Merrilee stood and Gus rose to her feet, as well. "I'll
see myself out."

Gus felt almost queasy as she stood in her den, listening to Merrilee's footsteps as she went down the stairs.
Even that sounded angry. She knew there was some
merit to Merrilee's concern, but Gus also felt Merrilee
was projecting some of her own issues onto Gus and the
situation with Nick. God knows, Merrilee had control
issues of her own in spades.

Gus drew a deep breath. That had been horrible. She exhaled, letting it go. Life wasn't static. Relationships changed. She and Merrilee might never be the same again, but they would mend this fence eventually. In the meantime, Gus was determined to enjoy this time out of her ordinary life with an extraordinary man. And if Nick proved her wrong, she supposed she would handle the consequences on her own.

11

MERRILEE DIDN'T KNOW WHAT to do. She sat at her desk in the airstrip, her stomach knotted with anxiety. She hated that things were on a sour note with Gus and to cap it, she was worried sick about her.

She couldn't talk to Bull about this. He'd already told her she had to stand back and let people make their own mistakes. But if she couldn't talk to Bull, she couldn't talk to anybody. Bull wasn't just her lover, he was her best friend, her confidante.

She shoved her chair away from her desk. Forget it. She was talking to him. She double-checked the flight schedules. It was a slow day. Near Christmas tended to be that way. They were either booked to the gills and both Dalton and Juliette were making runs or it was a nothing-going-on kind of day.

"Jeb, Dwight, I've got to go out for a bit," she said loudly to the two men who spent their days parked by the woodstove, playing chess, and arguing.

"Lights don't look out to me," Jeb said, glancing around at the Christmas tree and the overhead fluorescents.

"Huh? What was that?" Dwight asked.

They were both nearly deaf as a post. Merrilee had finally figured out they lip read one another, which was the only thing that kept them from perpetually shouting.

She stepped closer and repeated herself so they could read her lips. Both men nodded in sync.

She bundled into her coat, pulled on her winter boots, and stepped out into the midday light. It wouldn't last long. You'd think being from the South that the long winter days would make her melancholy, but she sort of liked it. But then again, she didn't need anyone to tell her that she'd always marched to her own drummer.

She passed Tessa's new video store and realized she should drop by to check on Tessa—just to make sure everything was coming together smoothly with her new business. She'd do that on her way back. Right now, she needed to talk to Bull.

The hardware store was empty and Bull sat behind the counter, a halogen light illuminating him and the charcoal drawing he was working on. The man had artistic talent out the wazoo. There was nothing he couldn't do.

He took one look at her, put down his charcoal, rounded the counter and wrapped her in a big bear hug. There was nothing quite as comforting in this world as a hug from Bull. She already felt a little better.

"What's the matter, honey? Tell me what's wrong."

She wasn't quite sure what she'd do without Bull or

how she'd gotten so lucky to find a man like him. "I want to tell you, but you have to promise not to fuss at me."

"The only thing I'm going to promise you is that I'm going to be straight up with you. Whether it's what you want to hear is another matter."

"Why don't we walk while we talk? I haven't seen the community center since they decorated it for the pageant tonight." And maybe the exercise and cold air would help clear her head. Plus, Bull would go a little easier on her if they were out in public. And that was a two-way street. If he made her really angry she wasn't as likely to say something she might regret later because she wasn't one for making a scene—it was unbecoming of the town founder and mayor.

"Then let's walk." Bull grabbed his jacket and hat and put them on.

They stepped out on the sidewalk and Bull offered his arm to Merrilee. She linked her arm through his. He always did that and she always liked it. They headed in the direction of the rectangular log building and Bull said, "It's Gus, isn't it?"

Merrilee nodded and waved at Perry as he passed by in his Suburban. "Nick came over and packed up. He's staying with Gus the rest of the time he's here."

Bull shrugged. "We all saw that coming. Those two were like a magnet and iron from the first time I saw them around one another. You should be glad she's finally found someone to have a fling with."

"But he could—"

Bull interrupted. "If he was going to, he already

would have, Merrilee. I happen to be a pretty good judge of character and I'd say he's a man of integrity."

Merrilee laid out for him just how much Nick knew, that he'd figured out most of it himself, and how, in her opinion, it was simply a matter of time before he deduced Troy's identity.

Bull simply nodded again, unruffled.

A gust of wind sent the snow skittering in front of them. "I'm afraid he's going to hurt her."

"Maybe."

"Maybe what?"

"Maybe he will hurt her. I don't think he would deliberately but it could happen. But I don't think that's what you're really afraid of."

Jenna waved at them from inside Curl's and they waved back.

"I have a feeling you're about to tell me what you *think* frightens me." She'd like to think Bull didn't know every nook and cranny of her soul.

"Sometimes a friend tells you what you don't necessarily want to hear. I think you're scared you're going to lose Gus."

"That's ridiculous," she responded automatically.

"Is it? You're a nurturer, Merrilee. You take care of everyone. Gus came here and she needed you. The town accepted her but she's never really made close friends with anyone else. She sort of keeps to herself other than spending time with you and me. I think Gus has taken on the role of the daughter you never had." Damn Bull. Gus was like the daughter she'd never had, could never have. She and Tad had never used birth control, nor had she and Bull, but a baby had simply never happened. "You're content here and you want her to be content here. But Nick is everything she left behind. I think you're not so afraid of her getting hurt as you are of him awakening her discontent with life in Good Riddance."

There was a hard-to-swallow ring of truth to his words. She *was* afraid of losing Gus who had become enmeshed so thoroughly in the fabric of Merrilee's life. "I didn't want to hear that but I needed to."

"I didn't think you'd want to hear it, but it had to be said."

As much as she didn't want to admit it, she knew Gus wasn't in full bloom in Good Riddance. But Merrilee had thought that given time… "She can't leave here. It's not safe for her out there with that nut job. If he finds her he'll do something terrible to her and men like that don't give up. You know he's still looking for her. At least if he finds her here, she's got all of us to protect her."

"There's a difference between her not being able to leave and you not wanting her to want to leave. There's a time and a season for everyone. Let Gus have her season with Nick."

"I don't always like what you have to say, but most of the time I need to hear it." She owed Gus an apology. She leaned up and pressed a kiss to Bull's cheek. "Thank you. Sometimes you do know me better than I know myself."

"That's why you love me."

Yes. Yes, she did.

GUS TOOK A SECOND TO SAVOR the rightness of Nick sitting stretched out on her couch with his laptop, working. She'd had no idea he wore glasses when he wrote. She thought the black-rimmed frames added to his sexy factor—not that he'd needed any help.

"I'll be back in about half an hour," she said. "If you want to go check out the cross-country skiing before then, don't worry about locking up."

"I'll probably still be working. I'm passing on that event. It's not quite the same as watching downhill where it's all right in front of you. You're closing the restaurant early tonight, aren't you?"

Gus grinned. "Yep, can't be open when the Ms. Chrismoose pageant is going on. And we'll close for the parade and the Mr. Chrismoose contest, which, incidentally, you have to enter."

"I wouldn't dream of missing it. It's part of the total experience, just like being a pageant judge tonight."

"Don't let that power go to your head."

"It's hard not to." He waggled his eyebrows. "I get to decide who'll wear the moose crown for the next year."

Gus opened the door leading downstairs. "Just remember absolute power corrupts absolutely." She closed the door behind her, muffling his laughter on the other side.

Gus couldn't remember a time when she felt more energized except for maybe when she'd just graduated from cooking school. Merrilee had come by with a hug and an apology. Not that she needed the older woman's blessing, but it was nice to have. Nick had moved his stuff over to Gus's apartment and was staying with her until he left. Granted they'd gone from zero to sixty, but when opportunity came a woman's way, she was stupid not to grab it with both hands before that opportunity walked back through the door. And there was something about living in Alaska that brought you to do the extreme.

Gus stopped by a couple of tables to say hello as she made her way through the restaurant. Once outside she beelined for Curl's, waving at Tessa on the way. Maybe she'd pick up a video for Teddy on her way back. Gus had called this morning to check on Teddy who was still down for the count. This flu was nasty business. Gus was doubly grateful she hadn't come down with it, since it would have been impossible to run the restaurant if she had the flu.

Nancy Perkins, who ran the dry goods store along with her husband, Leo, was coming out as Gus arrived at Curl's. Nancy held out her bright red nails for Gus to admire. "Don't they look great?"

Jenna had decorated each thumb nail with silver bells.

"Beautiful. Very festive."

"Leo loves red nails," Nancy said. "He says they turn him on." She winked.

That was more than Gus wanted to know about the retired insurance salesman from Wisconsin. Definitely cabin fever. "Then he'll be a happy man."

"Yes, he will. Have a great day."

Gus stepped into Curl's and the scent of nail polish greeted her. Jenna looked up from tidying her station and looked around as if to make sure no one was lurking in the corners, even though Gus and Jenna were the only two in the room as far as Gus could discern. "Did you bring it?" Jenna said in a loud whisper.

"Is there anyone in the back?" Gus asked.

"Well, no."

"Okay, then I think we can talk in our normal voices."

Jenna giggled. "Oh, right. So, you've got it?"

Gus sat in the chair across from Jenna. "Look, Jenna, we need to talk about this. No, I didn't bring it."

Jenna looked as if she'd just been told Santa Claus was a myth. "But…"

"Jenna, there's a couple of things wrong with that. First, it's just not safe to feed wild animals or try to attract them. But second, it either works between you and Nelson or it doesn't." She didn't know any other way to say it.

Tears gathered in Jenna's eyes and she looked down at the table between them. "You think I'm not smart enough for him, don't you?"

Her quiet, sad question tore at Gus's heart. "That's not what I think at all. I think there are lots of restrictions put on Nelson by his culture and his standing in his community as a shaman-in-training. I'm not so sure even if an animal marked you the way it did Tessa that it'd make a difference. In fact, I'm pretty sure it wouldn't. Nelson and Clint have different circumstances and are different people. You don't need a recipe, Jenna. You just need to invite Nelson over to your place for dinner and see how it goes."

"I'm a lousy cook," Jenna said, clearly on the verge of crying.

"Don't cry. *That*, the cooking, I can help you with. I'll hook you up with a take-out meal for two. Just tell me what you want me to prepare."

"For real?" She sniffled and blinked.

"For real." Gus patted her on the hand. "Just let me know when."

"What if I ask him and he turns me down?"

"Then you'll know, won't you?"

"Maybe I don't want to know for sure."

"That's a decision only you can make, but you know, Jenna, there's something very powerful in being the one who decides for themselves rather than having things decided for you. Just like you decided to dump Tad and stay here." Just the way Gus had decided she wouldn't allow Troy to keep her running. "Now you get to decide whether to ask Nelson over or not." Gus grinned. "Although I have a pretty good idea which way you're going to swing on that."

Jenna smiled. "Yeah, me, too. I'll let you know if I need that meal to go."

"I'll keep my fingers crossed."

"Better that than your legs." Jenna's smirk was all insinuation. "I heard Nick's staying with you for the rest of his trip."

Gus laughed. And she didn't even bother to ask how Jenna knew. "Yes, he is, so I'll just make do with crossing my fingers."

"He's a hottie."

Simply talking about him made her feel all warm and

gooey inside, like a cinnamon roll hot out of the oven and oozing glaze. "I noticed."

"But he's not as hot as Nelson."

She'd beg to differ all day long but to each her own. Gus stood, smiling. "I'll leave on that note. Let me know how it goes."

"You'll be the first to hear."

Gus walked out the door, leaving Jenna beaming hopefully behind her nail station. Gus hoped Nelson didn't break Jenna's heart. He wouldn't on purpose but sometimes life's circumstances meant that two people couldn't be together.

Sad, but true.

"Hey, we have alone time together and it's not even midnight yet. Mark it on the calendar," Nick said as he pulled Gus closer to his side on the couch. He liked touching her. He liked spending time with her.

"I know, it's pretty amazing," she said with a laugh. "That's what closing for the Ms. Chrismoose pageant does for you."

"The pageant was fun," he said. "Although I have to tell you, being a judge is a little bit of pressure. No, make that a whole lot of pressure."

Gus smirked. "Dalton and Clint tried to warn you. But no…"

"You have absolutely no idea how relieved I was when they told me all the little girls would be named Little Miss Chrismoose princesses. The idea of having to just pick one and disappoint all the others…"

Gus nodded. "I know. This is the first year we've had

the Little Miss Chrismoose part. They were all so cute up there."

"Yeah, they were, weren't they?" He could just see her getting her own little dark-haired daughter ready for the pageant one day. It gave him a funny feeling inside. "You like kids?"

"I do, although I've never spent a lot of time around them. I was an only child so I've never had any nieces or nephews like you do."

"There's plenty there, if you wanted to borrow one or two."

She laughed. "I'd say ship them on over but I think their parents might protest. Come to think of it, the kids would probably protest, too."

"Are you kidding? They'd be fighting over who got to come. They would think you were totally cool."

"Really? You think they would?"

"My nieces would all want to be just like you and my nephews would all be moonstruck just like their uncle."

"Moonstruck? And here I was thinking it was lust-struck."

He grinned. "Well, that too. So, do you want children?"

She toyed with the pleat in her pants. "Sure. One day. I always wanted several. I guess it's that only-child syndrome."

"Um, how many is several?"

"Well, three or more. But if you say a couple then that means two so I always opt for saying several."

"What about your career?"

"I'd manage," she said. "Well, we'd manage, me and the dad. People do all the time. Your parents did."

"True enough."

"What about you? Or have all those nieces and nephews given you cold feet?"

"No, I'm all for wading into the gene pool when I find the right woman to swim with." And he wasn't so damn certain he wasn't looking at her now. He certainly had never felt this way about anyone else.

She laughed. "That's one way to put it."

"I've been told I have a way with words."

Nick wasn't sure how deliberate it was when Gus changed the subject. "I'm glad Skye won. Apparently Dalton harassed her into participating. She didn't think she stood a chance in the first place, but especially considering her red eyes from working such long hours."

Skye's mouth had dropped open when her name was called. But the best part was when the town doctor gave a whoop. The whole room had erupted in cheering and laughter. "She seemed pretty excited. There were more people there than I expected."

"It's not as if there's an abundance of entertainment in Good Riddance," Gus pointed out on a dry note.

He found her comment both interesting and telling. Did she know how much she'd just revealed? "I had noticed."

"Up until this year we had the pageant at the airstrip center because the participants could change upstairs, but people were crammed in like sardines. Wait until the Mr. Chrismoose contest tomorrow and the parade the next day. Everyone will turn out for those, too. The fishing derby and races are pretty well attended but no one misses the contests and parade."

"Do you close the restaurant for both of those events?" He hoped she'd be there and not working.

"I do for the parade. The whole town shuts down and turns out so it's pretty pointless to be open."

"Pretty nice to have some time off of work, isn't it?"

"Tonight was my break. Lucky gets the parade break since it falls during lunch. I love having the restaurant but the odd days off are certainly welcome."

"That's what I always saw with my parents. They love cooking and they loved being in the restaurant business but they were pretty much married to it. They never took a vacation together."

"Really? I think if you have the right staff in place it's doable. I could leave Lucky in charge and it'd be fine for a couple of days, probably even a week."

"I never thought about it that way. I just thought they couldn't but you know, both Mom and Dad have this attitude that no one else can do things quite as well as them. It's not arrogance, I think it's just a control issue."

"How long did they have the restaurant?"

"Thirty-five years. They sold it last year."

"Do they miss it?"

It had been a hard decision for them and at first they'd thought they'd made a mistake but it had worked out in the end. "I think they did at first but they help out with my nieces and nephews, and since my sisters and brother live on the same street but they all work, Mom and Pop cook a big dinner almost every night and everyone eats at their house."

"Sounds like fun." There was a wistful note in her voice and Nick realized what he'd taken for granted— both parents and a big extended family. He had no doubt they'd love her and she'd love them.

"Chaos," he said, thinking of everyone talking at once at the big table that could seat a small army. "It's pure, utter chaos…but yeah, it's a good time."

"I'm sure Christmas is fun there, as well. I bet you're looking forward to it."

An idea had been playing in the back of his mind all day. He wanted more time with her. He wanted the opportunity to see if what he was feeling was real. He figured the worst she could do was say no to his proposal, so he tossed it out there. "How would you feel about me changing my ticket and staying through Christmas?"

She looked away from him, to the small tree standing in the corner of her living room, and he was all but certain she was about to tell him no.

"I think I'd like that." She turned back to face him, her expression not revealing what she was thinking. "How will your family feel about it?"

Was she looking for an out? If so, he wasn't going to give it to her. If she didn't want him to stay, she'd have to point-blank tell him. "There have been a couple of Christmases I didn't make it home. They'll miss me but it'll be okay. My sisters and brother will be there, along with their crews."

A slow, sweet smile bloomed on her face and lit her

eyes. "Then I'd love to have you here for another couple of days."

Relief swept through him. He'd really wanted her to say yes. "Good, 'cause I'd like to stick around. I'll see if I can change my ticket to the twenty-seventh. Does that work for you or will I have worn out my welcome by then?"

"I think it'll be fine. Where's your next assignment?"

"Greece. I leave the second week in January."

"There are worse places to be than the sunny Mediterranean in January while the rest of us are freezing our tushes off."

He laughed and nodded. "Exactly what I was thinking."

"Teddy will be thrilled you're sticking around. She's been lamenting being sick the entire time you've been here."

"What about you? Are you thrilled I'm sticking around?"

She slid onto his lap and wrapped her arms around his neck. "I'm okay with it."

12

THE NEXT AFTERNOON GUS WAS IN the kitchen menu-planning and putting together a supply order when Merrilee dropped in. "Thought I'd stop over while it was quiet and your hip attachment was out at the dogsled races."

"Very funny. He's excited about the Mr. Chrismoose competition and the cook-off." Gus always gave the cook-off a wide berth after she'd figured out she made the contestants nervous.

"I like Nick's enthusiasm. He's interesting but better yet, I think he's a good guy and those come in short supply."

"What? Are you actually coming around, Merrilee?" Gus asked, teasing her. Then she sobered. "He is a good guy."

"He seems crazy about you. I thought it was pretty telling when he decided to stay for Christmas."

"It'll be nice to have him here."

"Gus, you're not being cooperative at all. I'm trying to find out how you feel about Nick."

Gus laughed. She knew exactly what Merrilee was up to and was just teasing her. "Obviously I like him."

"Honey, how are you going to handle it when he leaves? Because the longer he stays, the harder it's going to be when he leaves."

She didn't even want to think about it. How she felt about Nick had been all tangled up from the beginning but the more she got to know him, the more intense she felt about him. Last night with all their talk about kids and families and then when he'd asked to spend Christmas with her, she'd thought she was in real danger of being in love with him. However, in the cold light of day, she'd realized you couldn't possibly love someone you'd only spent five days with. Quite simply, she was infatuated with him. Who wouldn't be?

"I'm not looking forward to him leaving," she said, "but that's been a given from the very beginning—a ship passing through."

Merrilee, a frown creasing her forehead, was about to say something when Jenna walked in the restaurant's front door. The blonde fairly skipped across the floor. "Guess who's coming to dinner. Guess who's coming to dinner," she said in a singsong voice.

"Dwight and Jeb," Gus said. The two old-timers who hung out over at the airstrip office blushed every time Jenna said hello to them. It was pretty cute.

"No, silly. Nelson. He said yes. Hey, Merrilee." She gave Merrilee a quick hug. "You look pretty today."

Gus had noticed Jenna always had a nice word for everyone.

Merrilee glanced from Jenna to Gus and back to Jenna. "Nelson's coming to your house for dinner?"

"I know. Can you believe it? Thanks so much for telling me to ask him, Gus. Now, can you make dinner for me? If you tell me what pans you need I'll bring them over."

Merrilee shot Gus a surprised look. "You told her to ask him to dinner?"

"Long story. Later." Gus turned back to Jenna. "How about a lasagna with salad and bread?"

"That sounds perfect."

"But you have to make dessert. You can't fake the entire thing."

Jenna looked positively panicked. "But I told you I can't cook."

Merrilee looked more confused than ever.

"I'm Cyrano de Bergerac-ing the meal for Jenna," Gus explained to Merrilee.

Now it was Jenna who appeared confused.

"What are you going to do to the lasagna?"

"Never mind. It will be fine and you'll be fine on dessert because you can follow directions. Go by the store and pick up a brownie mix. It's super easy. Grab some ice cream and chocolate sauce and you can make brownie sundaes for dessert. If you want to go fancy, sprinkle some nuts on top."

"You're the best, Gus."

"I don't know about that, but I'm glad you think so. Now when is this dinner taking place?"

"Tonight. He's coming over at seven."

Tonight? And Jenna was just telling her *now?* If it had

been anyone else… However, Gus knew it was a matter of Jenna being spacey rather than thoughtless. It'd be tight but she'd swing it. "No problem but I'm going to need a pan from your place."

"Which one?"

"You know what, honey," Merrilee spoke up, "don't worry about it. I'll run next door and grab one from my kitchen. I'm not going to need it for the next couple of days."

"For real? You're the best, too, Merrilee."

"Thanks. I'll go get it. You got any appointments this afternoon?"

"No. Everyone wanted morning appointments. No one wants to miss the Mr. Chrismoose."

"Tell you what. It's a slow day for me, too, so why don't I walk down to Leo and Nancy's with you for that mix and then keep you company while you're cooking."

"That would be great!"

Gus knew exactly what Merrilee was up to. It was anything but a slow day for her since she was always swamped during the festival, but she was going to make sure Jenna's brownies turned out well. Merrilee really was the best.

THAT EVENING, GUS LOOKED around in satisfaction. The bar was humming and she was getting a break. The evening of the Mr. Chrismoose competition, where the men competed in a series of events such as ax throwing and sled pulling, was always a much bigger alcohol than food night. The men were still pumped up from the games and were much more interested in drinking as they ribbed one another and inflated their own performances. One year a fight had broken out but for the most part it was all in good fun.

Nick, working behind the bar, was taking his fair share of ribbing. He'd been a good sport and jumped right in there with the others. She suspected he'd hammed up his ineptitude just to provide comic relief.

It would be far, far too easy to get used to having him in her life. She reminded herself once again to enjoy the moment because the day was coming soon enough when he'd be gone. He looked up and caught her watching him. His grin got even bigger and he boldly winked at her across the way. Gus laughed and shook her head.

She couldn't remember when she'd laughed as much as she had since he'd arrived. He'd turned to pull another beer when her woolgathering was interrupted.

"Gus? Can I talk to you?" Jenna's red-rimmed eyes told the tale.

Poor Jenna needed some privacy, not to be standing in the middle of Gus's place. "Come on," Gus said, "let's step into the stockroom. It's back here."

As soon as the door closed behind them Jenna began to cry.

"Oh, honey, I'm sorry," Gus said, putting one arm around Jenna's shoulders.

"You were right," Jenna said, swiping ineffectually at her tears. "I could be marked up one side and down the other and it wouldn't matter."

Gus pulled a couple of napkins off the shelf and

passed them to Jenna. "I was afraid that was the case."

"Thanks." She blotted at her face. "And I came clean on the dinner. I confessed that I can't cook. And do you know what he said?" Tears began to leak from her eyes again.

"What?"

"He said whether I could cook or not wouldn't matter when I found the right guy." She hiccupped. "Why does he have to be so sweet when I can't have him?"

"That was very sweet...and true. Oh, honey, you'll meet someone else." The minute the words left her mouth, Gus realized it wasn't likely anytime soon. Look how long it had taken her to find Nick and he was on a temporary basis.

"But I don't want anyone else. Why did we have to be star-crossed lovers?"

Gus didn't have any ready, pat answer for that. "I don't know, Jenna. Sometimes people just can't work things out past their circumstances." As was the case with her and Nick. She couldn't leave Good Riddance and he couldn't live here. So, where did that leave them?

It left them going their separate ways in a few days.

Jenna nodded in resignation and gave her nose a final blow. "But you know what? I'm glad I did this tonight. Even though this isn't the way I wanted things to work out, you were right. It is better to decide something for yourself than have it decided for you. I'm gonna go home now and go to bed."

"I promise you, it'll be better in the morning after a good night's sleep."

"Thank you for everything. You're a good friend and you give good advice."

After Jenna was gone, Gus realized maybe it was time she started taking the advice she'd dispensed so freely. She was going to take her power and wield it. It wasn't enough to not run from Troy. She needed to stop him. Tonight she'd tell Nick Troy's name and she hoped like hell he could bring the Wenhams down or at least Troy. The idea of having to face him again nauseated her, but she would do what she had to do. Troy would no longer control her.

NICK'S GUT TOLD HIM SOMETHING was up with Gus as they climbed the stairs to her apartment. He'd just been getting this vibe from her all during the cleanup routine. "Is everything okay, Gus? I'm just getting this feeling..."

She opened the door at the top of the stairs and he followed her into her apartment. When she turned to him, there was a tinge of sadness to her smile. "You know me too well," she said.

Closing the door, he said, "Talk to me."

"That's what I want to do. I have something to tell you."

O-kay. "You want to sit down? You want us to go to the bedroom?"

"The couch is fine." They sat next to one another and he waited. When she was ready, she'd say what she had to say. She knit her fingers together and squared her shoulders. "Nick, my real name is Lauren Augustina Matthews." She took a deep breath. "I know you would've figured it out on your own before long but it's important to me that I'm the one who tells you. His name is Troy Wenham."

Nick instinctively whistled under his breath. "Wenham? *The* Wenhams?"

"Yes. The Wenhams."

He reached over and placed his hand over hers. "Thank you for telling me. I think I know how much that took for you to do that." Something niggled at the back of his mind. He was pretty sure...but he wasn't about to tell her that without verifying his facts first.

"I want you to do whatever you can with the information, Nick. I want to make it clear I'm not asking you to sit on this. If you think there's a story and you can bring them down, blow the lid off."

"You are one hell of a woman, Lauren Augustina."

"I'm glad you think so."

He was already reaching for his laptop. "Look, I need to check something on this guy."

"I'm going to pour myself a glass of wine. Do you want one?"

He was pretty damn sure that while she might've told him Wenham's name, she wasn't ready yet to watch while Nick looked him up. "Sure. I'll have a glass."

Gus moved into the kitchen and within seconds he was online. Another few seconds and bingo, information confirmed. He picked up the laptop and sprinted into the kitchen. "Put the wineglass down—" he didn't want her to drop it when she saw the screen "—and take a look at this."

She shook her head, "Nick, I don't—"

"Oh, yes, you do." He put the laptop on the counter and turned her to face it.

"Oh, my God," she breathed.

The headline screamed Wenham Declared Lost at Sea.

"He's dead, Gus. He was honeymooning on a cruise when he went missing. No foul play was ever proved but it had been suspected he'd had some help over the rail. I thought I remembered it from when it happened but I wanted to verify it before I told you."

"He's dead," Gus said in an almost-monotone voice.

"Almost two years," Nick said, unsure of what to say or do. He couldn't gauge how she felt. She just looked blank. True the guy had sent her into hiding, but she'd also cared enough about him at one point to be engaged to him. Nick was a little out of his emotional depth here.

Gus began to shake. "He's dead. I never have to be afraid of him again."

Nick wrapped his arms around her, drawing her close, offering whatever comfort and strength he could. "No. He's permanently gone."

"I never looked. I tried not to even think about his name so I never looked," she said against his chest. He smoothed his hand over her hair.

"You okay?"

"I'm so relieved I could cry and that's just wrong to feel good about someone being dead."

"No. No, it's not wrong at all to feel that way when you consider what he took from you and put you through.

You had to give up a life you loved and start all over. Don't waste even a second feeling guilty."

"I know it's late but I need to tell Merrilee and Bull. They've been through this with me and I want them to know. You don't have to, but I'd like for you to be there when I tell them. If it weren't for you, I wouldn't know. I might have never known."

"I'd be honored to go with you."

Gus glanced at his laptop. "Would you mind bringing that, too? I want her to actually *see* it and *read* it."

"I understand." And he did. There was an inherent confirmation in the written word. He scooped up his computer. "Let's go."

GUS DIDN'T KNOW HOW TO FEEL. Troy was no longer a threat. She'd lived in his shadow for so long, she hadn't even realized how heavy the weight had been.

"You okay?" Nick asked yet again.

How had a man as thoughtful and great as him stumbled into her life?

"I'm better than okay. I'm just still trying to absorb it all," she said. Gus opened the door and they crossed into the airstrip office. Upstairs Merrilee and Bull were obviously moving around. She'd called Merrilee. Luckily Bull was over spending the night and Gus had asked them to meet her and Nick downstairs.

"Why don't you set your laptop up on Merrilee's desk?" Gus said.

Nick had just finished when the older couple came downstairs—Merrilee with a lace-trimmed flannel robe knotted at her waist and Bull in jeans and a flannel shirt but barefooted.

"Come look at this," Gus said without any preface.

Merrilee took one look at the headline, cut her gaze to Gus, then back at the computer screen and promptly burst into tears. She enveloped Gus in her arms, squeezing her tight.

"That's the best damn news I've heard in a long time," Bull said.

Merrilee released Gus and wiped at her eyes with the edge of her robe. "I second that." She moved over to the computer screen and bent down. "I need to read this. I know you shouldn't be happy to hear that someone has passed but I'm beyond happy."

"I told Gus she shouldn't feel guilty about feeling that way." It was the first thing Nick had said since Merrilee and Bull had entered the room.

"You were obviously behind this. Let me just say I'm damn glad you showed up in Good Riddance," Bull said.

Merrilee straightened. "I second that, too. I owe you an apology."

Nick shook his dark head. "No, you don't. You didn't know me and you wanted to protect Gus. No apology necessary."

"You set her free," Merrilee said softly. "If you hadn't shown up..." She trailed off, shaking her head.

"That's the same thing I said," Gus said. "If Nick hadn't shown up then I might have never known. I was never going to go out looking for him."

"Me, either," said Merrilee, "'cause just thinking about him made my skin crawl."

"Well, I have to admit the internet might actually be good for something after all," Bull said.

"Lost at sea," Merrilee said and then harrumphed. "I bet someone pushed his sorry ass overboard."

"Actually, they think his new bride did but they could never prove it. When Gus told me his name I thought it was the same guy but I wanted to confirm it. There was a big stink."

Gus's stomach clenched to think what the other woman must have gone through to drive her to push Troy overboard. "I hope she's happy now."

"Ya know what? She's free, the same as you are, so I'm sure she's happy...or at least happier than she was with him," Merrilee said.

Yes, she was free. It was a heady, heady feeling. And suddenly it seemed as if she was so light she could sprout wings and fly. She felt as if she could smile all night. And speaking of all night...

"I'm sorry I got you out of bed but I didn't think it could wait until the morning."

"Are you kidding? I would've been upset with you if you hadn't gotten us up to tell us this. In fact, do you have any champagne next door?"

"It's seldom called for but I always keep a bottle cold." Perhaps it was macabre to toast another person's demise but that was precisely what they were going to do. "C'mon, let's go."

She was free.

13

MERRILEE LAY IN THE BED and watched the digital clock, wide-awake. Beside her, Bull snored quietly, his sleep clearly uninterrupted by rumination. The Chrismoose festival had ended the day before and all the visitors had cleared out of town. In a few minutes it would be Christmas day. Things were back to normal, yet they weren't.

She had never seen Gus so happy. Merrilee hadn't truly understood what a dark cloud the girl had lived under until news of Troy's death had lifted it. And she suspected Nick's presence in Gus's life might have a little something to do with her constant smile these days. She hoped Gus would find the kind of happiness with Nick that Merrilee had found with Bull now that Gus was free of Troy's control, just as Merrilee was free of Tad's control.

She issued a quick, silent prayer of thanks for her blessings and for Bull in particular. He had been the greatest blessing in her life. She'd bought him a new whittling knife that was now wrapped and sitting under the tree. She thought he'd like it. It wasn't that he particularly needed a new knife but this year she'd really struggled with what to give him for Christmas.

She knew what he really wanted. His words, "I get to call you my wife" had replayed in her head a thousand times since he'd uttered them. She truly, deeply loved the man beside her but Tad had so soured her on marriage....

It wasn't as if a lightning bolt struck her. Rather, her realization actually came to her quietly. She was all kinds of a fool. Tad was still controlling her. He continued to run her life, influencing her decisions, primarily her decision not to marry Bull.

She sat up in bed and gathered her courage. It was 12:02 a.m. Christmas Day. She reached over and shook Bull's shoulder. Nothing. The man slept like the dead. She shook harder. "Bull. Wake up."

He sat up, shaking his head. "Huh? What it is? What's going on?"

She pointed to the clock on the dresser. "It's Christmas Day."

"It's also just after midnight."

"I wanted to give you your present."

"Merrilee, the knife can wait until the morning. Yes, I know it's a knife—I found the receipt when I was looking in your drawer for a stamp." He lay back down and started to roll over but she stopped him with her hand to his shoulder.

"You're a pretty smart man, Bull Swenson, but you don't know everything. I didn't wake you up to give you that knife. You can just sit right back up and quit being grumpy."

He issued a long-suffering sigh but sat up regardless. "Okay."

She climbed out of bed. Dang but the floor was cold.

"Now what are you doing?"

"I'm trying to do this right," she said as she rounded the end of the bed to his side.

He was running low on patience and she was afraid she might run low on nerve so she acted quickly. Without further ado, she dropped to one knee and took his hand in hers.

"Bull Swenson, will you do me the honor of becoming my husband?"

His hand trembled in her grasp and his eyes bored into hers. "If this is a joke, it's not funny, Merrilee."

"I would never joke about this, Bull. You told me the asking would be up to me, so I'm asking."

"You're sure?"

"Never surer."

Merrilee was fairly certain everyone in Good Riddance heard him whoop, but instead of sealing her proposal with a tender kiss, the crazy man jumped out of bed past her, leaving her still kneeling. He hurried over to his dresser, yanking open one of the drawers.

"What in the name of heaven are you doing?"

"Getting this," he said, turning around with a jewelry box and envelope in his hand.

Turning on the bedside lamp, he knelt down on the floor beside her and she figured they must've truly looked like two old fools. He thrust the box into her hand. "Open it. Go ahead. Open it."

She lifted the hinged lid and gasped. Nestled in velvet, one of the prettiest rings she'd ever seen winked in brilliance. "It's beautiful...and huge. When did you get this?"

"About twenty-five years ago. Just before the first time I asked you to marry me."

"You've had this for twenty-five years? And you never said anything?"

"You never said yes, but I figured sooner or later you'd come around. It's certainly been a damn sight later." He plucked it from the box. "Well, try it on."

She held out her hand. "You put it on me."

"Don't mind if I do," he said, sliding the ring onto her finger. He brought her hand to his mouth, pressing a tender kiss to the back.

Tears threatened Merrilee and she blinked them away. "It fits perfectly." She turned her hand one way and then the other, admiring the way it looked.

"I had it resized last year, you know when you gained a little weight and you had to have your other rings sized up."

"Well, the ring is perfect," she said, getting to her feet. Her knees couldn't handle kneeling on that cold floor. Nor could Bull's. "We can talk about setting a date in the morning."

He rose, shaking his head, a sly grin on his face. "We've already got a date."

"How can we have a date when we haven't even discussed it and I'm the bride?"

"Because we're getting married today."

"Today?" She started laughing. "We can't get married today. We have to plan and send out invitations and get a license."

"The hell you say. We're getting married today after the Christmas service." He tapped the envelope he'd pulled out of his drawer. "Here's the marriage license."

"When did you get that?" She held out her hand for the envelope. Sure enough, it was a marriage license.

"I got it the day Tad signed those divorce papers."

"But—"

"There's no but to it, Merrilee. I'm hitching my wagon to yours today before you can change your mind."

Any other words of protest died on her tongue. He'd waited for her for twenty-five years. She wouldn't ask him to wait any longer. "Okay. We're getting married today."

Bull climbed to his feet and crossed to the bedroom window. Raising the window, he leaned out into the early Christmas dark and bellowed, "Merrilee Weatherspoon is going to marry Bull Swenson today after the Christmas service. Everyone's invited." He ducked back inside and slammed the window closed. "Someone surely heard that so by morning it'll be all over town."

Merrilee laughed with delight. "You're crazy."

"Yes, I am—crazy about you."

"ARE YOU NERVOUS?" Gus asked Merrilee as they waited in the church's vestibule. Spruce boughs hung with big, fat red velvet ribbons adorned the doors and scented the air.

"No, honey, I'm just happy. Once I made up my mind and popped the question, well it just felt too right to be wrong."

"You look beautiful," Gus said. "Absolutely beautiful."

"You really think so?"

"No. I know so." Merrilee was radiant in a soft rose flannel dress trimmed at the collar and cuffs in ecru lace. Jenna had come over earlier in the day and given Merrilee a manicure/pedicure as a wedding gift. "I'm so happy for you, Merrilee."

"Thank you, honey. I want you to be happy, too."

"I am. I certainly am."

"Life is funny the way it seems to come full circle. Your mama stood up for me in my first wedding."

Gus had known that but she'd forgotten. The reminder brought tears to her eyes.

"Well, I'm honored to be here now."

"Your mama would be so proud of you. She was always proud of you."

"Thank you." Gus's throat thickened and she swallowed hard. She would not cry.

Tessa cracked open the door. "It's time," she said. She'd volunteered to photograph the wedding.

Merrilee nodded and Tessa opened the double doors. The church was packed. Every seat was taken and people stood between the end of the pews and the windows. Even the choir area behind the pulpit was crammed with people.

"Okay, kid, lead the way," Merrilee said.

Gus had been incredibly touched when Merrilee had asked her to stand up as her maid of honor. But she'd been beyond surprised when Bull had asked Nick to stand with him as best man. Bull's reasoning was Merrilee could ask Gus because she was family but if Bull asked any of the local men, someone was sure to get their nose out of joint and feel slighted over not being picked. So, he'd chosen the out-of-towner, Nick.

Gus started down the aisle ahead of Merrilee. Bull and Nick waited at the other end. She'd never seen Bull in a suit before. But it was Nick she couldn't seem to stop looking at and he seemed to be in the same fix.

It was almost as if everything and everyone else faded away and it was simply her making the trek down the aisle to him. It seemed that every day, every hour her infatuation with him grew and deepened. It was a good thing he was leaving day after tomorrow or she would be in serious trouble.

She deliberately looked away. Reaching the front of the church she took her spot opposite Bull and Nick and watched as Merrilee made the same trip. You could almost feel the love and devotion passing between Merrilee and Bull.

The ceremony was short but sweet. Merrilee had wanted to write their own vows and Bull had stubbornly clung to the traditional. They'd compromised with a hybrid. The traditional ceremony was interspersed with a couple of lines Merrilee threw in.

More than once Gus's gaze seemed to tangle with Nick's during the vows and the exchange of rings—Bull had possessed the foresight to buy his own ring all those years ago, as well.

Mack Darcy, who'd gotten his nondenominational ministerial license through an internet course, wore a big, ear-splitting grin when he said, "You may kiss your bride."

Bull, quiet but strong Bull, who was always the rock in the background, wrapped his arm around Merrilee and laid one heck of a kiss on her in the front of that church before God and everyone. When he let Merrilee go, she was flushed. She fanned herself and said loud enough for everyone to hear, "My goodness. I should've married you years ago."

Mack said, "Ladies and gentlemen of Good Riddance, I now present to you, Mr. and Mrs. Bull Swenson."

The church erupted. Everyone stood. There was clapping, shouting and whistling as a beaming Bull and Merrilee made their way back down the aisle.

Gus leaned over to Mack. "Hey, folks, hey," he practically yelled to be heard over the noise. The crowd quieted a bit, enough for him to announce, "There's a reception for Bull and Merrilee over at Gus's for everyone who wants to come. They understand if you have other plans on Christmas day."

Nick appeared at her side, offering his arm. "I believe it's traditional for the best man to escort the maid of honor."

She slipped her arm through his. "I believe you're right."

They started down the aisle and gooseflesh prickled her skin. This felt so natural—walking down the aisle of a church, linked with Nick. She reminded herself she was just being sentimental and emotional. Nonetheless, it still felt achingly right and she couldn't seem to stem the smile on her face. From the end of one pew, Jenna gave her a big thumbs-up. Next to her, Dalton, with Skye by his side, shot the two of them a knowing smirk.

Nick chuckled. He'd seen them, as well. "They're a good group of people."

"Yes, they are."

Clint was waiting outside in his Suburban, the motor running, to take Nick, Gus and Tessa over to the restaurant ahead of the crowd. Nick and Gus piled in the back, while Tessa took the front.

"That was wonderful," Tessa said.

"Yes, it was," Clint said. A look passed between him and Tessa, tender and private. Gus deliberately looked out the window so as not to intrude on their moment. Nick took her hand in his, intertwining his fingers with hers. She looked at him and what she saw in his eyes literally took her breath.

"Everybody ready?" Clint said.

Gus dropped her gaze, breaking eye contact with Nick, but he didn't relinquish her hand. "Ready."

"I understand you've got the spread laid out," Clint said as he pulled onto Main Street.

"Gus is amazing," Nick said. "You won't believe what she pulled together this morning."

Merrilee had called her early with the news, wanting Gus to hear it from her first. Once she got off the phone, she'd hit the ground running, and Nick had run right along with her, pitching in and helping organize.

"It wouldn't have happened without everyone's help."

A pale, but recovering Teddy had shown up along with Mavis. Luellen, Tessa, Jenna and Donna had all come knocking, offering to help decorate and do whatever had to be done. Nelson had dropped in long enough to set up the karaoke equipment and then promptly disappeared. He, Skye and Dalton were up to their own mysterious plans.

Tessa grinned from the front passenger seat. "Honestly, it was like one of those chef challenges on reality TV. where they have to pull something together in a certain amount of time."

Gus laughed. "It was, wasn't it? And we couldn't have scripted it any better if we'd tried."

Leo and Nancy Perkins, the dry goods store owners, had shown up with an entire wedding reception package of high-end paper plates, plastic champagne flutes, streamers, confetti and the honeycombed white paper wedding bells you unfolded and then taped together.

Years ago Elmer Watkins, the same one who'd croaked in Gus's restaurant, had mail-ordered a bride and a wedding package. The bride had developed cold feet and was a no-show. The reception paper goods, however, had been delivered on time. They'd been sitting at Leo and Nancy's, dust collecting on the plastic shrink wrap, for years. The only thing Gus had elected not to use were the napkins with *Elmer and Daisy, June 2, 1990* embossed in gold foil. They'd make do with plain white cocktail napkins.

And then there'd been the surprise call from Curl.

"Who would've ever guessed that Curl was sitting on a case of champagne over there?" Gus asked.

"It was the damndest thing I've ever seen," Nick said with a chuckle. Curl had called with the offer but he was still down with the flu. Clint had swung by, picked up Nick, and the two of them had headed over to get the bubbly. "There's this room that's refrigerated and there are tables obviously there to accommodate bodies, either animal or human, and in the corner is a case of champagne."

"Not just any champagne either," Gus said. "It's Cristal."

Tessa, Nick and Gus all exchanged knowing looks. Clint simply looked lost. "Never heard of it."

Reaching over, Tessa patted Clint on the arm. "Unless he stole it—" they all knew she was making a joke "—he dropped a couple of thousand dollars on that case. It's nearly three hundred dollars a bottle."

Clint whistled. "Whoa. I'll sip slowly when we toast today, then. We won't be serving that at our reception, will we, honey?"

"No worries. We'll be pouring the cheap stuff." Tessa laughed, then looked over her shoulder. "But I definitely want you to cater it, Gus."

"Absolutely. Just give me the date."

"Tessa's been working with Nelson and Grandmother to figure out the best time for us to marry to ensure a happy union." There was no mistaking the pride in Clint's voice.

Tessa was about as blond and green-eyed as they

came, but there was no doubt in Gus's mind the woman possessed a native soul.

"Just let me know when."

Nick spoke up. His hand, still clasping hers, tightened. "If you let me know the date, I'd like to come back for that. And Dalton and Skye's wedding, too."

"Oh, my God," Tessa said. "A man volunteering to attend a wedding." They all laughed and she grinned at Nick. "I'd love to have you at our wedding."

"Me, too," Clint said.

Gus felt all funny inside. So, he was planning to stay in touch obviously. She'd thought come day after tomorrow he'd simply ride off into the sunset. She wasn't so sure that wouldn't be the easier course of action.

They pulled up in front of the restaurant. She'd have plenty of time to contemplate her life without Nick soon enough. For now, she had a wedding reception to host.

14

"YOU THROW A HELLUVA reception, honey," Nick said, slipping his arms around the most amazing woman on the planet.

"*We* threw a helluva reception. I'd like to remind you that you pretty much single-handedly prepped all of the hors d'oeuvres while I worked on the cake. I can't thank you enough for your help. I seem to have said that a lot this past week."

"We make a pretty good team, you and I."

"We do, don't we?" Her smile never failed to move him.

"So much for your day off."

"You know, as the boss, I'm making an executive decision. Gus's is closed tomorrow. I'll call Lucky, Mavis and Teddy and put a sign on the door."

"You'd do that?"

"Watch me. You're leaving day after tomorrow. I'd like one day with you without Chrismoose or the restaurant or even something as wonderful as an impromptu wedding reception."

"I'd like that too."

"I'll make the calls. You make the signs."

While she was on the phone he dug out paper and a marker from behind the bar where he'd seen them earlier in the week. By the time she got off the phone, his handiwork was finished.

"Okay. They were all happy as clams to take tomorrow off, especially since they all pitched in today. You've got the signs ready?"

"Here you go," Nick said. "One for the front door. One for the airstrip door."

She read the sign and squealed. "Nick Hudson. You are bad."

"I told you I had a way with words. And for a guy, I've got fairly decent handwriting."

He'd neatly printed: *Gus and Nick are upstairs making love all day. Please come back tomorrow. Sorry for any inconvenience.*

"Give me some thumb tacks. They're in the junk drawer below the register."

"You're not really going to put them up? It was just a joke."

She grinned. "It's not as if that's not what everyone will think anyway. I've had a reputation as a saint for way too long."

Something very primal in him surfaced. Jealousy, plain and simple. He neatly tore the papers into halves and then tore again. "Oh, hell no. I don't want to think about every man within a five-hundred-mile radius beating feet to your door once I've gone. There'd be a line circling the block."

He quickly wrote: *Closed today. Will reopen tomorrow. Sorry for any inconvenience.* "Here you go. I'll make another one while you put that on the front door."

She laughed at his reconsideration but took the new sign nonetheless. "In all the activity I forgot. Did you talk to your family today?"

"Yeah, I went upstairs for a few minutes and called."

"Did you miss being there?"

"Are you kidding? Today was incredible. There's nowhere I would've rather been. Nothing else I would have rather been doing. And, most importantly, no one I'd rather have been with."

He'd never been surer of anything in his life. It was just like his parents and siblings had said it would be. She'd started down that aisle today and it had all just clicked into place for him. He loved her. She was the one meant for him.

THE NEXT DAY, GUS STRETCHED, feeling thoroughly decadent and thoroughly satisfied. "I can't tell you the last time I was still in bed at noon."

Nick grinned and kissed the end of her nose. "It's not a common occurrence for me either, but this could be habit-forming."

He rolled to his side and climbed out of bed, naked. She liked him naked. She liked him most any way, but naked really, really worked. Unfortunately, he decided to change that state and pulled on a pair of underwear.

"Don't get dressed on my account."

He grinned over his shoulder as he reached for a pair of jeans. "This is on the account of not shocking the citizens of Good Riddance. I've got to run out for a minute."

"Where?" she asked before she thought. Really, it was none of her business except she'd just assumed they'd stay sequestered in her apartment all day. And where the heck was there for him to run out to here?

He sent her another one of his heart-thumping grins. "I'm going to pick up some bagels and cream cheese."

She laughed. "Right. Did Santa bring that to the corner deli on his sleigh yesterday?" So he didn't want to tell her where he was going. That was fine.

He tugged on his shirt and pulled on socks. His boots were by the door in the living area. "He just might have. I won't be gone long. And please, definitely do not feel obligated to put on any clothes in my absence. I like you naked."

"Funny. I was just thinking the same thing about you."

He leaned down and gave her a thorough goodbye kiss. "Hold that thought."

Then he was out the door whistling under his breath.

"Shall I make some coffee to go with those bagels and cream cheese?" she yelled out behind him, going along with his ridiculousness.

"Nah. Let's do champagne instead."

"Okay. You're picking that up along with the bagels?"

"Yes, ma'am, I am."

She heard the outer door close behind him and she laughed, rolling over onto her belly, burying her face in his pillow. She inhaled his scent. That was just one of the things she loved about Nick, his playful sense of the absurd. Well, not loved...make that liked in the extreme.

There were just too many factors playing into it for her to think she was really in love. She'd had a fangirl crush on him years ago, he was the first man she'd been with in over four years, he'd bailed her out of a tight spot professionally when Teddy got sick, and he was the one who'd delivered the news Troy was dead. Not to mention he was drop-dead gorgeous, smart, funny and fantastic in bed. Those all just muddied the emotional waters. So, yes, she was infatuated beyond belief but...

Her phone rang and she thought about ignoring it but couldn't. "Hello."

"Honey," Merrilee said, "I hate to bother you but there's something you've just got to see. Go look out your front window. I'll stay on the line while you do."

"Okay." Gus rolled out of bed and snagged one of Nick's shirts thrown over a chair, pulling it on. Looking out the window naked didn't strike her as a prudent move.

"You there yet?"

"Almost. How was the honeymoon?"

Merrilee giggled on the other end. "Wonderful. I highly recommend it."

"Okay. Now what am I looking for?"

"Dalton. In the sky."

About the time Merrilee said it, Gus saw it. Dalton

was doing a flyby, a banner trailing behind the plane that read, *Congrats 2 Bull & Merrilee Swenson.* Gus laughed with sheer delight. *That's* what Nelson, Dalton and Skye had been up to yesterday. "That is so cool."

"Isn't it? He requested clearance to fly this morning and then told me I needed to step outside. That boy is something else."

"Skye and Nelson were in on it, too, I'm pretty sure."

"Definitely."

Gus looked down at the town and a set of familiar broad shoulders caught her eye in the midday light. What was Nick doing going into Curl's? She shook her head, thoroughly perplexed.

"I'll let you go. I hope you're enjoying your day off. I was glad to see your closed sign."

"I am enjoying it." Even though she had no clue what Nick was doing. Truth be told, Gus was a little hurt he'd interrupted their day, when they had some of the hard-to-find privacy that was so rare in Good Riddance, to be out running around town.

"Gus…"

"Yes?" Still at the front window, she saw Nick walk back out of Curl's, a definite spring in his step. What the heck? She stepped away from the window. "I'm sorry, Merrilee, I was distracted for a minute there. What were you saying?"

"I'm just going to share something with you that my very wise husband told me not too long ago. There's a season for everything, Gus. Just remember that, a season for everything."

Still somewhat distracted by why Nick would've popped by Curl's, Gus answered absently, "That's lovely, Merrilee."

"Lovely isn't the point, honey. Take what it means to heart."

"I will."

They got off the phone and Gus wandered into the bathroom. She'd just finished brushing her teeth and running a comb through her bed head when she heard the door open.

"Honey, I'm home," Nick called out.

"Got those bagels and champagne?"

"Sure do. Plus cream cheese and lox."

Shaking her head—he had consistency in a joke down pat—she walked out of the bathroom…and stopped in her tracks. There was no mistaking the fragrant pungency of onion bagels. Dumbfounded she said, "You picked up bagels."

"I've been telling you that." He pulled a bottle of Cristal from under his arm. "And champagne." He winked at her across the room. "I snitched a bottle yesterday and put it away."

She started laughing and then couldn't seem to stop. He was without a doubt the most impossibly charming, romantic man she'd ever encountered…and was ever likely to.

"I'm glad you're amused. Now go back to bed so I can bring you breakfast in bed."

She just stood there, still sort of dumbstruck. Where in the world had he gotten bagels, lox and cream cheese?

"Begone with you, woman. Go. Bed. Now. I'll be there, in a minute."

She went. She took a minute to smooth the sheets and fluff the pillows before she climbed back in. God help her, if she hadn't been totally besotted before, she certainly was now.

Within a few minutes he came through the door, everything arranged on a wicker breakfast tray. "Merrilee," he said by way of explanation for the tray. "You didn't even notice it when I came in, did you?"

"No. I was so blown away by the bagels."

He placed the tray at the foot of the bed and made quick work of stripping down to his underwear. "Can't get into bed wearing clothes."

"Certainly not. That's a vast improvement."

He climbed in next to her and his weight on the mattress nearly upended the tray. He caught it just in the nick of time. "Damn. This stuff never happens in the movies."

Gus giggled, she simply couldn't help herself. "That's because it's the movies and sometimes life's just messy. I take it you don't have a lot of experience serving breakfast in bed."

"This is a first."

That would explain why he'd left the brown bag on the tray, but she thought it was sort of cute. "Well, you're doing just fine."

"How about some champagne?"

"You should be ashamed of yourself. This was supposed to be for the reception yesterday."

"Then I say our first toast is to Merrilee and Bull."

"Open it, you incorrigible man."

The cork flew across the room and he quickly poured the fizzing pale liquid into two glasses, handing her one. "To Bull and Merrilee's long-awaited nuptials," he intoned.

"To them." They clinked stemware and then took a sip. It was seriously good champagne.

"Now, a second toast. To us." His eyes, his words, seemed to pierce to her very soul.

"To us." For whatever reason, this sip tasted even sweeter, more effervescent than the first.

"How about a bagel?"

"Okay, put me out of my misery. Where did you get onion bagels?"

His grin turned her heart upside down. "There's a little deli on the corner about a block from my apartment, Zimmerman's. I made a phone call. Two-day air is a beautiful thing."

She held the bagel to her nose and inhaled, closing her eyes. "Ah, a true New York onion bagel. Have I died and gone to heaven?"

"I'm guessing you're a lox fan."

She was. An onion bagel with cream cheese and lox was to die for, but it meant some seriously heinous breath. "Are you going to have some, too?"

"You betcha."

They sat together, contentedly munching and drinking their way through a bagel and another glass of champagne. Gus wasn't sure whether it was the food, the drink, the company, or a combination thereof but she felt positively giddy.

"Hey, Gus, would you mind checking the bag? I think there's another cream cheese in there."

"Sure." She put her glass on the nightstand and picked up the small brown bag. "There's...something..." She reached in and her fingers closed around a band. She pulled it out. A ring. A diamond ring. Was this...did this mean...? She turned to him and stupidly said, "There's no more cream cheese."

"I know the ring is used. I bought it off of Jenna. We'll get you another one, one we pick out together, but I didn't want to get on that plane to leave tomorrow without a ring on your finger."

She was in shock. She felt as if she was moving in slow motion in a dream. "That's why you went to Curl's."

He shook his head. "Truly. There are no secrets in this town, are there?"

"I was looking at Dalton's banner and saw you."

"It doesn't matter. I love you, Gus. You're the one I want to go swimming with. You're the one I want to wade into that gene pool with."

She just sat there stupidly, trying to take it all in. She hadn't expected...never anticipated... Whoa.

"I've traveled lots of places, met lots of people. I can't say I've dated lots of women. I told you, I'm not a casual kind of man. I just always knew when I met the right woman, that I'd know. That's what it's like in my family. It was that way with my parents, both my sisters and my brother. When I saw you walking down that aisle yesterday, I knew."

"Nick, I don't know what to say. This is so sudden."

"I love you, too, would probably be a good place to start."

She couldn't. She wished she could, she really did, but she couldn't. "I have very deep, very strong feelings for you."

Despite the disappointment registering in his blue eyes, he smiled. "Well, that's at least a good beginning. I don't think you're a casual woman any more than I'm a casual man."

"No, I'm not." She was reeling. "I just never thought you'd consider moving to Good Riddance. Do you really think you'd be happy here? I think you'd be bored within a month."

Now it was his turn to look shocked. Well, not exactly shocked, but she didn't imagine the look of surprise on his face, in his eyes.

"No, I don't think I belong in Good Riddance. And I don't think you do, either. I think New York is in both of our blood. I think that's where we belong."

He was serious, which left her all the more incredulous. "I have a business, my own restaurant. This is my home we're sitting in. Those people out there, the ones you've spent the last nine days with, those people are my family. You heard Tessa yesterday. I'm going to cater her wedding. But you expect me to just give all of that up? To just walk away so that I can start all over again while you give up nothing?"

"Gus, I would walk away from my job, my family, the city—and you damn well know what all of those mean to me—to be here with you if I believed, if I thought this was where you really belonged, but, honey, it's not. You ran and this was the only place to go and you've done your damnedest to make it work, but it's not you. You don't like the long, dark days. I'm ninety-nine percent sure you've never gone hiking, hunting, or fishing. There's not a thing about you that says wilderness living."

"The only family I have in the world is here."

"My family will love you. They'll love you because of who you are and they'll love you because I love you."

She was already shaking her head. "I can't. I won't."

"Tell me one thing. Do you love me?"

"I don't know how I feel about you." She looked at the brown bag.

"Can you sit there and tell me you don't love me?"

She opened her mouth but the words wouldn't come. "No, I can't tell you that, either."

"I'm not rich, but I make decent money and I'm not a big spender. I've got a nest egg socked away. I don't know how much capital it takes to open a restaurant in the city, but we'll look into it."

Dammit. He was going to make her cry. Why did he have to be so sweet? Why didn't he grow impatient and yell? Once again, she shook her head. "When my mother died, she left me money. It's in a trust fund. Once I disappeared I couldn't possibly touch it without Troy finding me. I'm not rich either, but I'm not destitute. I don't want your money."

"I've seen the work you do, the kind of ship you run. Some people have tremendous talent in the kitchen but no business or organizational sense. You have the gift of both. I told you days ago that your talent was too big for Good Riddance. I would willingly invest in any food enterprise you were part of, whether we're together or not. And I don't invest my money lightly."

"Thank you. That means a lot to me." She pushed the ring to his side of the tray. "I can't take this ring."

He left it where it lay. "It's yours, Gus. I don't need it. I'm not looking for another woman. I'm not Wenham who's trying to control you or stalk you. I'm more your Bull Swenson variety of man. I've found the woman I want so I'll wait. Bull held on to a ring for twenty-five years. You hold on to yours. I hope I'm not waiting that long, but if that's what it takes… My mother always says good things come to those who wait, and I can't think of anything better than you."

15

"DID YOU EVER TRY THE RING ON?" Nick said the next morning as he finished packing. He had gone out of his way the rest of yesterday and last night to keep their time together light.

She hesitated and then smiled sheepishly. "I did. It's jewelry and I'm a woman. What can I say?"

"Did it fit?"

"Hold on." She opened her nightstand drawer and pulled out the ring. She slipped it onto her ring finger on her left hand. God, he was pathetically in love with her because that was it. If he couldn't leave with an "I love you" or any kind of promise, he could at least see what the ring he'd given her looked like on her hand.

"It fits perfectly," she said. She held out her hand to show him.

"It's not what I would've picked out for you, given an actual jewelry store selection, but it looks good."

"I like it. I just don't...I can't...."

"I know. It's okay."

"How did you know Jenna had a ring?"

"My first evening here she offered to sell it to me if I needed one before I left." He shrugged. "It turns out I felt like I did."

"I'm not going to even ask about that conversation."

He laughed. "Skye and Tessa were warning me what happens to poor unsuspecting fools who show up in Good Riddance. It turns out they were right." He zipped his travel bag.

He hated to bring it up, but they had other unfinished business they needed to discuss. "Gus, I need to know, what do you want me to do about the Wenhams?"

It was her call. He'd play it the way she wanted him to play it. Exposé stories weren't really his thing but if she wanted them brought down, he'd dig and pull it together and make it stick.

"I don't want to impact your career, but all I wanted was to stop Troy and he's stopped. Yes, the Wenhams enabled him but even though he was wrong he was their son and they loved him. They've been punished."

"You're telling me to let sleeping dogs lie?"

"Essentially, unless pursuing this would really further your career. As I said, I don't want to stand in your way."

"You've read enough of my work. This isn't my career direction. It'll go no further than here."

"Okay." She tugged the ring off. "I wish you'd take this."

"No. It's yours. It was a gift." He grinned. "You're a woman and it's jewelry. So, I guess I'd better head next door. Dalton's flying me into Anchorage."

"What time do you get into New York?"

"With the four hour difference I'll make it back in time for dinner tonight at Mom and Dad's."

"Will everyone be there?"

"Oh, yeah. The whole crew."

"Got any plans for New Year's Eve? Any parties?"

Nick had the impression that now it was time for him to leave, she was stalling because she didn't want him to go.

"We all get together at my folks' house. What about you? Do you keep the bar open?"

She smiled. "Yep, it's our one late night out of the year. And then we're closed on New Year's Day."

He nodded as the alarm on his watch sounded. He turned it off. "I've got to go."

"I'll walk over with you—"

"No. I'd rather you not. Let's just say au revoir here."

"Nick, thank you for—"

He didn't want her to thank him, dammit, he wanted her to love him. He interrupted her with a hard, thorough kiss.

"When you're ready to swim with me, I'll be waiting."

He opened the door and stepped into the dark, bracing cold.

"Travel safe," she said softly behind him. He simply nodded. He couldn't turn around and look at her because he wasn't sure he could actually walk away if he did. He heard the door close behind him.

When he walked into the airstrip office, it was warm, toasty and just as damn cheery as the first time he set foot through the door. Was it only nine short days ago? His entire life had changed in that span of time.

Merrilee looked at him, her hopeful expression fading when she realized he was alone. He merely shook his head. Of course, before he'd even made it back to Gus's yesterday everyone had known he'd bought Jenna's ring off of her.

"Give her time, Nick. I know she loves you. I recognize it when I see it. Same as I know you love her."

"I do. I think I fell for her the first time I caught a glimpse of her through that door."

"She's just scared. Scared to trust herself. Scared to trust you."

Nick laid it on the line. "I want her to come to New York. She doesn't belong here."

"I know that, son. I didn't want to acknowledge it for the longest time, but I know that. She's stifled here. I know it. You know it. Now, she's got to figure it out. Give her time."

Nick felt an unutterable sense of relief. With Merrilee backing him…the woman was formidable and he'd damn sure rather have her as an ally than an enemy, having been on both sides of that particular fence.

"I told her I'd be waiting. I just hope it doesn't take twenty-five years."

She swatted at him. "Get out of here." She winked at him. "We'll all make sure it doesn't."

Gus put off going down to the kitchen until the very last minute. Tonight's menu was simple and easy, requiring very little in the way of prep time. She'd used the extra time to scrub her apartment from one end to the other. She'd tried a couple of times to strip her sheets off the bed to throw them in the washer and found she couldn't do it. She wasn't ready yet to erase his scent from her bed. No one but her needed to know that. And then she'd spent a ridiculous, inordinate amount of time looking at that stupid ring.

She went downstairs and found Lucky hanging out in the kitchen, talking to Teddy. "Hey, Gus, I was waiting on you to come down. I wanted to talk to you about something."

"Sure. Go ahead," she said as she tied on her apron.

"I want first dibs on buying the place."

What was he talking about? "Buying what place?"

"Here. Your place. Gus's."

"But it's not for sale."

"Well, I figured with you moving back to New York—"

"I'm not moving back to New York."

Lucky scratched at his head, clearly perplexed. "Nick's moving here? No offense, he's a nice fella and all but he doesn't belong here anymore than you do."

"Thank you. Thank you very much, Lucky."

He looked at Teddy. "What? What'd I say wrong?" He looked back at Gus. "I told you I thought he was a nice fella. Just promise me you'll think about it."

"I'll see you in the morning, Lucky."

Gus and Teddy worked in merciful silence for a while after Lucky's exit. Gus fumed silently. Of all the nerve, him saying she didn't belong here.

"Gus…"

"Yes?" Teddy wasn't usually so tentative.

"I was wondering…well, you know it's my goal…"

First Nick had left. Then Lucky had lost his mind. Her patience was wearing thin. "Just spit it out, Teddy."

"Well, I was thinking if you moved back to New York maybe next year when I move, you could sort of help me find a place and show me the ropes since we know one another and stuff and I won't know anyone else there, well, except for Nick, now."

It all came out in one long sentence without Teddy pausing for breath, and Gus realized Teddy had spent the last twenty minutes working up her nerve to say that.

Gus counted to five and prayed for patience. She couldn't snap at poor Teddy. "Teddy, *if* I were moving back to New York, of course I would mentor you. I would insist on it. But—"

"Are you serious, Gus? That would be so awesome and Marcia would feel so much better about me going if somebody from our hometown was looking out for me."

Oh, boy. "I said *if,* Teddy. I'm *not* moving to New York."

"But why not?" Teddy looked at Gus as if she was an alien species.

Gus was mercifully saved from answering Teddy by Jenna prancing through the door. "Okay, let's see it."

Gus looked at her blankly. "See what?"

"THE RING. Hel-lo."

"I…uh…I'm not wearing it."

"Well, why not? You should be able to cook in it.

You're wearing that ring," Jenna said, pointing to the black onyx on Gus's right hand.

"I'm not wearing it because I'm not engaged."

"But why not? I know he asked you, that's why he wanted to buy the ring...and by the way, he paid too much for it."

"He asked. I said no." If it was anyone other than Jenna, who was one of the sweetest people she knew, she'd tell them it was none of their business but she couldn't hurt Jenna's feelings.

"I don't get it," Jenna said. "He loves you. You love him."

"I didn't say I loved him."

"You don't have to." Jenna looked at Teddy and rolled her eyes. "Duh. Anyone can see it."

Jenna, of all people, should understand. "Jenna, remember that talk we had about how sometimes two people just couldn't be together because of circumstances?"

"Yeah, star-crossed lovers. Uh-huh."

"Well, that's me and Nick. I live here and he lives in New York. See, it's the same situation."

"Gus, I know a lot of people think I'm an airhead and sometimes I don't quite catch everything, but I've got to tell you, *that* is the dumbest thing I ever heard." Okay, Gus had just hit an all-time low. "I can't change my DNA, but duh, all you have to do is pack up and move."

"It's not that simple."

"Yes, it is."

"No, it's not."

"Gus, I just did it. I should know." Jenna giggled. "And I didn't even pack up. I just showed up with a suitcase and stayed. There hasn't been anything hard about it."

"But I have a business here."

"What do you think I did back in Georgia, spend all my time shopping?" That was precisely what Gus had assumed. Thank goodness the question had been rhetorical as Jenna barreled on. "I own a beauty supply store franchise. I just have a good manager in place." She wrinkled her nose. "How'd you think I could afford to live here on what I make doing nails at Curl's?"

"I…uh, hadn't really thought about it." And talk about a lesson in not judging a book by its cover.

"And before you tell me your friends and family are here, I left mine back in Georgia. But everyone here's real nice and I like it. I've already made lots of good friends." She stopped and thought about something for a few seconds, a frown wrinkling her brow. "Unless people don't like me and I don't know it."

Gus shook her head. "I don't know of anyone who doesn't like you, Jenna."

"Oh, good. Oops. I've gotta run. Mavis is coming in for an acrylic full-set. I just got all my fake nail stuff in yesterday and I am *booked*."

Lucky and Jenna had merely portended things to come. Clint and Tessa came in for dinner and Tessa stopped by. "Gus, Clint and I have been talking about a summer wedding, probably July. You know we want you there but do you think you could come back a day early so you could still cater it?"

"Tessa, I told you the other day I'd cater it."

"I know, but now that you're moving to New York…"

"I'm not moving to New York."

"When did that happen?"

"I've never been planning to move."

"Oh. I just thought…never mind."

All through the evening, people stopped her to wish her well, telling her to keep in touch, asking for enough notice so they could throw her a farewell party.

The final icing on the cake was when someone played Sinatra's "Theme from New York, New York" on the jukebox and everyone in the damn room turned to look at her. When had that been loaded on the jukebox?

She'd had it. Stick a fork in her. She was done.

Gus marched over to the table where Dalton, Skye, Tessa, Clint, Nelson and Jenna were all gathered. "Nelson, would you please turn on the sound system, primarily the microphone?"

"Sure."

She followed him to the small raised stage and in a minute he had her hooked up. Walking over to the jukebox, she yanked the plug out of the wall, cutting Frank off in mid-refrain. It was as if she'd pulled the plug on everyone's conversation. She had their attention now.

Gus stood on the stage and said into the microphone, she wanted to make sure everyone heard her loud and clear, "Hope everyone is enjoying their dinner tonight." There were lots of nods and murmured agreement. "Good. Now I need everyone to start spreading some news. I don't know how the rumor got started, but I'm *not* moving to New York. I'm staying right here in Good

Riddance." Several people throughout the room shook their heads as if they didn't quite know what she was thinking. "That was it. Enjoy your dinner."

The conversations resumed and the room was back to normal. She handed the microphone back to Nelson. Nelson regarded her solemnly with his dark eyes. "The loons and many other birds fly south for the winter. They know when the season has passed, if they stay where they don't belong, they will die."

Gus didn't say a word. She simply walked back to her kitchen. This evening couldn't end soon enough.

TWO DAYS LATER, Gus marched over to the airstrip office and plopped down in the extra chair next to Merrilee's desk. She'd had it. "Why is everyone suddenly trying to get rid of me? For three days now, everywhere I go, everyone I see has something to say about me leaving."

"Everyone just wants you to be happy, Gus."

"But I thought everyone liked me here. I consider them extended family."

"Nature's got it figured out, honey. When I was a girl, my grandmother Danvers used to plant zinnias—you probably don't even know what those are."

Gus shook her head.

"They're kind of old-fashioned flowers. They're all different colors and they're just wonderful. They attract butterflies and they make good cutting flowers. So, my grandmother had these wonderful zinnias that came back year after year because they reseed themselves."

Dalton poked his head in the door. "Hey, Gus. Morning, Mrs. Swenson. I'm heading out to Carlisle now."

Merrilee beamed at the salutation and nodded. "Got it. Be safe."

Dalton ducked back out the door and Merrilee continued, "So, one year, I must've been about nine, Grandmother Danvers gave me a seed packet of my own zinnias so I could enjoy them at my house. She came over and showed me right where I needed to plant them because zinnias require full sun." Merrilee shook her head. "Even then I was a stubborn little cuss. I wanted to plant them where I could see them from my bedroom window. That spot didn't get full sun but it got some sun so I thought it'd be okay. Anyway, my seeds came up and I had a few blooms but overall the plants were spindly and just sort of sad sack. My plants were just barely surviving. Grandmother came over, told my head a mess, and stood there and watched me while I dug up every one of those poor plants and transferred them to where she'd told me to plant them in the first place."

"And they thrived."

"I had the prettiest zinnias all summer long. They went to town when they were where they belonged."

She got the analogy, but it hurt. Merrilee, of all people… "And you think I don't belong here."

"Honey, I love you as if you were my own. You're like the daughter I was never blessed with and I wanted you to thrive here, but you were a forced transplant and you've survived but it's the wrong conditions for you. Nick knew it from the beginning. I want you to thrive, Gus. I want to see you bloom and grow to your fullest potential. Troy uprooted you, now it's up to you to transplant yourself back where you belong."

"It's not just that, Merrilee. The whole thing with Nick... How can I trust it? How can I really feel this way about a man I've known for just a little more than a week?"

"I fell in love with Bull the minute I saw him. Then I spent the next twenty-five years waiting for him to prove he wasn't the man I thought he was. He is. Take it from an old woman, good men are hard to find in this world and when you find one, honey, you better hang on to him. Nick's a good man."

She wanted to trust it but she couldn't. She'd already made one huge, life-altering mistake. "But I thought Troy was a good man, too. And look what happened there."

"Did you really? Or were you a little blindsided by the fact that he was a Wenham? And weren't you lonely still with no family and missing your mama? You aren't in the same place emotionally now that you were then, Gus. You've had some hard seasoning. You're wiser, more discerning, and you have a whole bunch of people who care for you. Trust yourself."

"Merrilee, it's been sort of crazy and I've been distracted but I never did ask you, why'd you finally decide to marry Bull? What changed your mind?"

"I figured out I was still letting Tad Weatherspoon yank my strings and control me."

Gus didn't get it. "But—"

"Because Tad left me with such a sour taste in my mouth on marriage, I wouldn't marry Bull. I decided I wasn't letting that man drive any more of my decisions."

Nodding slowly, Gus said, thinking aloud as much as anything, "Troy drove me here and I'm still letting him keep me here. This isn't just about Nick, it's about me. I can't be part of his life until I've worked out who I am and where I belong."

"That's why he wouldn't move here. Not because he doesn't love you and not because he's being selfish about his family and his job. If he moved here, he'd just be enabling you to continue to cripple yourself."

"How'd you get so smart?"

"It's the same school you're attending, honey, the school of life and hard knocks."

IN THE MIDDLE OF THE AFTERNOON on New Year's Eve, Nick paced the limited space in his apartment one more time, wishing he'd just stayed in Good Riddance through the end of the year. Maybe if he had and they'd started the new year together, that would have sent Gus a message. Maybe if he'd stayed a little longer she'd have gotten past those fears that held her back.

Hell, he'd even thought about hauling his butt back across the continent to show up for the occasion. He'd checked the flights and been one click away, but then he'd reconsidered. She needed space and time. He couldn't force her, he couldn't rush her, and he sure as hell didn't want her to think she had another stalker on her hands.

He'd plopped onto the couch and reached for his laptop when there was a knock on his door. No one ever dropped by his apartment but his younger sister Lisa had said earlier she might stop by. Why she needed to come by when he'd see her tonight at Mom and Pop's was beyond him, but whatever.

He hauled himself off the couch, threw the locks on the door and flung it open. No Lisa. Gus. *"Gus?"*

"Hi." Her smile was tentative, as if unsure of her reception. "I was in the neighborhood and thought I'd drop by. The office said you were working from home today." He was still dumbstruck. "Um, do you think I could come in?"

"Of course." Did this mean what he hoped it meant? "I'm just…yeah, come on in." He stepped aside. And then he saw it. The ring. She was wearing his ring on her right hand. He wasn't sure exactly what the hell was going on, but they were going to be okay because Gus was wearing his ring.

She twisted the ring on her finger. "I figured some stuff out. One biggie was that I do love you."

That was it. That was all he needed to hear. He scooped her into his arms and kissed her, welcoming her home, welcoming her into his life.

"What else did you figure out?" he asked when he finally came up for air.

Smiling, her arms linked around his neck, she said, "I want us to take it slow."

"Not twenty-five years slow?" He grinned.

"A little faster than that, but I don't want us to rush into anything."

Nick led her to the couch and sat down, pulling her onto his lap. He traced the curve of her cheek with his finger. "I told you before. I'll wait for you because you're worth the wait."

Her eyes echoed her earlier declaration of love. "I'm going to look for an apartment here in New York." He didn't offer for her to move in with him. She had this figured out and she had to move forward on her own terms. "Mavis and Lucky are going to run Gus's with the understanding that it may be Lucky's at the end of a year. In that year, I'll continue to have a share of the profits, which will mean some income while I look at putting my own place together here. And I always have the option of going back to Good Riddance in the meantime."

"A safety net? An escape valve?" It wasn't a criticism. Given her past, he totally understood her need, her rationale.

"Exactly. It was my escape once before."

"What made you change your mind?"

She laughed. "A whole bunch of stuff about seasons and plants and everybody and their brother all but pushing me out the door. But ultimately it was me figuring out that I no longer belonged there. It just took me a little longer to see what everyone else did."

"I'm glad you did. It's an understatement to say how glad I am that you're here. I can't tell you how many times I thought about going back to bring in the new year and hopefully a new start with you."

She shook her head and pressed a kiss to his cheek. "I had to do this on my own."

"I know. That's why I'm still here." He grinned evilly. "You know you have to go with me to my parents' tonight and meet everyone."

"How will they feel about a stranger coming in to a family gathering?"

"You're not a stranger. They've heard all about you. They already love you."

Her shy, sweet smile tugged at his heart. She shifted on his lap, linking her arms around his neck. Nuzzling his collarbone, she said, "What time do we need to head over there?"

"Hours yet," he said, following her train of thought. "Can you think of anything to do in the meantime? We could go shopping for another ring."

She looked at him askance. "Are you kidding? This ring has a great story and history behind it." She smiled. "I'm never giving it up, just like I'm never giving you up."

He grinned, happy that she liked the story that would become their story. "In that case, I've got an idea or two. I was thinking we could maybe go swimming together."

"I can't think of anyone I'd rather go swimming with," she said, sealing it with a kiss.

* * * * *

*Harlequin Presents® is thrilled
to introduce the first installment of
an epic tale of passion and drama by*
**USA TODAY Bestselling Author
Penny Jordan!**

*When buttoned-up Giselle first meets
the devastatingly handsome Saul Parenti,
the heat between them is explosive....*

"LET ME GET THIS STRAIGHT. Are you actually suggesting that I would stoop to that kind of game playing?"

Saul came out from behind his desk and walked toward her. Giselle could smell his hot male scent and it was making her dizzy, igniting a low, dull, pulsing ache that was taking over her whole body.

Giselle defended her suspicions. "You don't want me here."

"No," Saul agreed, "I don't."

And then he did what he had sworn he would not do, cursing himself beneath his breath as he reached for her, pulling her fiercely into his arms and kissing her with all the pent-up fury she had aroused in him from the moment he had first seen her.

Giselle certainly *wanted* to resist him. But the hand she raised to push him away developed a will of its own and was sliding along his bare arm beneath the sleeve of his shirt, and the body that should have been arching away from him was instead melting into him.

Beneath the pressure of his kiss he could feel and taste her gasp of undeniable response to him. He wanted to devour her, take her and drive them both until they were equally satiated—even whilst the anger within him that she should make him feel that way roared and burned its resentment of his need.

She was helpless, Giselle recognized, totally unable to withstand the storm lashing at her, able only to cling to the man who was the cause of it and pray that she would survive.

Somewhere else in the building a door banged. The sound exploded into the sensual tension that had enclosed them, driving them apart. Saul's chest was rising and falling as he fought for control; Giselle's whole body was trembling.

Without a word she turned and ran.

Find out what happens when Saul and Giselle succumb to their irresistible desire in

THE RELUCTANT SURRENDER

Available January 2011 from Harlequin Presents®

HARLEQUIN®

A Romance

FOR EVERY MOOD™

Spotlight on

Classic

Quintessential, modern love stories
that are romance at its finest.

**See the next page
to enjoy a sneak peek from
the Harlequin Presents® series.**

MARGARET WAY

Wealthy Australian, Secret Son

Rohan was Charlotte's shining white knight
until he disappeared—before she had
the chance to tell him she was pregnant.

But when Rohan returns years later as
a self-made millionaire, could the blond,
blue-eyed little boy and Charlotte's heart
keep him from leaving again?

Available January 2011

COMING NEXT MONTH

Available December 28, 2010

HBCNM1210